WALK IN THE SKY

Winner of the Edith Busby Award

WALK
IN THE SKY

———

JACK ISHMOLE

———

DODD, MEAD & COMPANY

NEW YORK

*The characters portrayed in this book are
fictitious and any resemblance to real
persons, living or dead, is entirely coincidental*

ISBN: 0-396-06512-0

Library of Congress Catalog Card Number: 74-38522
Printed in the United States of America
by The Cornwall Press, Inc., Cornwall, N.Y.

To Max Glück

It is not strength, but art, obtains
the prize
And to be swift is less than to
be wise . . .

—Homer

. . . They have assumed the names and gestures
of their enemies, but have held on to their
secret souls . . .

—N. Scott Momaday
from *House Made of Dawn*

1

THE TELEVISION SET flickered its pattern of colored lights through the darkened living room where Mike Montagne, ironworker, sat like a prehistoric caveman fascinated by the fire in front of him. He had turned the volume up loud, the way he liked it, and the voices and canned laughter coming from the set pounded their way through the rooms of the old brownstone house, as though quiet was an enemy to be banished. Out of the living room, through the kitchen in the rear, up the staircase, bouncing against the walls and doors, and then back again to where Mike sat. His large, powerful frame filled the comfortable club chair, and his feet, still in work boots, covered the small hassock. One hand was busy dredging up the last of the potato chips, feeding them automatically into his mouth, while the other hand reached for his second can of Schlitz. He was oblivious to the crumbs falling to his lap. The figures on the television screen seemed to have hypnotized him, commanding him to emit an occansional raucous laugh.

TV VOICE: Ugh! He wentum thataway. Me thinkum you havum heap big trouble.

2ND TV VOICE: Little Bull, why you thinkum we havum trouble?

TV VOICE: If we no havum trouble, Bald Eagle, we no havum program.

(CANNED AUDIENCE LAUGHTER)

"That's a good one," said Mike. He often talked to the television set as though he were part of the program. It was called "Wild Woolly West," and since its debut three months before, it had conquered all of its competitors for the important ratings which would insure a long and successful future.

During the first commercial Mike walked through the swinging door to the kitchen. He was furious to discover there was no more beer in the refrigerator.

"Why the hell do they do this to me?" he muttered to himself, rushing out of the kitchen to the hallway.

"Joey!" he shouted.

Upstairs, a door opened, and Joey shouted back. "I hear you. I'll be right down."

"Hurry it up!" Mike bellowed, rushing back into the living room, slamming the large, old-fashioned parlor doors shut.

In his room, where he had been trying to escape from the program, Joey Montagne had told himself—I am so damn tired of it all! Tired of Mike . . . King Mike the Boss. Tired of his voice, tired of his idiotic laugh, tired of his cigars and smoke, and that pure unadulterated junk he insists on watching.

For about an hour, Joey had been rehearsing the songs he would be performing the next evening. But the noise from the living room had made it almost impossible for him to hear the delicate shadings and chords of his guitar. Once, he had shouted down to his uncle to lower the volume, but Mike either had not heard or chose to ignore his request. Knowing that he had lost the battle against Mike and the electronic babble that had penetrated through the house, Joey had stopped his rehearsal when the first dull pain of a headache throbbed its way into his consciousness. He lay down on the cool sheets of his bed, hoping the pain would last only a short while.

For as long as they lived together, with Mike dominating life in the house on Schermerhorn Street in the North Gowanus section of Brooklyn, Joey knew he would have to resign himself to the constant arguments and the headaches. Old Papa Montagne, his grandfather, had willingly conceded the role of head of the household to his Uncle Mike, and Lily Montagne, his mother, was too busy taking care of the large house and its occupants to notice how naturally Mike had slipped into the crown and sceptre of King Mike.

—Who does he think he is? He is not my father. He could never replace my father in a million years. Somewhere in that thick head of his, he's gotten the idea that he is supposed to take my father's place.

The dull pounding changed into leaden pain. Each slight move made the pillow alive with invisible demons pulling and stretching every nerve and vein in his head. He got up very slowly and walked into the bathroom to get some aspirin. The sound of the cool water running into the glass made him think of open spaces, away from the house and Mike.

"Joey, where the hell does your mother keep the extra

beer? I told her a hundred times not to run out of it," Mike shouted.

As Joey walked cautiously downstairs, he knew he was not ready for the battle that would take place.

Passing the living room, he heard the canned laughter mixed with Mike's animal laugh.

—Idiots. They deserve each other.

He entered the kitchen, and after looking for a six-pack in a few likely places, remembered that he had seen his mother put one outside, on the back porch. He brought the carton inside, tore the cans loose, and placed them in the refrigerator.

—I hope he likes his beer lukewarm, because that's just what he's getting.

"Joey, you out there? Did you find the beer, or are you goin' out to get me some?"

—I have it right here, Chief Pain-in-the-Ass. Would you like me to pour it for you, right over your big, thick head?

Joey pushed slowly through the swinging doors. The room was filled with the sickening odor of stale cigars, and Joey stood transfixed, not wanting to see Mike, or to speak with him.

"What are you standing there like a dummy for?" Mike asked.

"Here's your beer," Joey said.

"You're not doin' me a favor, are you kid? What does a a guy hafta do around here to get a cold can of beer?"

"Maybe when a guy sees the supply running low, he replaces it before it runs out." Joey couldn't hide his annoyance.

"Don't give me any of your lip, Joey. If I ask you a decent question, I expect a decent answer," Mike barked.

"Does that work both ways, Mike? If I ask you a decent question?"

"Like what? I got no time for your questions."

"Like, why are you such a sucker?"

"Joey, you're asking for it . . . and one of these days you're gonna get it." Mike shifted his weight in his chair.

Joey wondered if he had gone too far. He turned away from the TV screen to the mantel over which Papa Montagne had hung some Mohawk heirlooms he had brought with him from the Caughnawaga reservation in Canada so many years ago. The rich, faded earthen colors of a drum, a set of rattles, a False Face mask, and a cradleboard stood out boldly from the white brick background. Other homes might have other decorations, but Joey liked the ones his grandfather had chosen. They were more than just decorative; they were a reminder of the past, of a time when the Montagne family had gone by another name, Hawk-of-the-Mountain, before the missionaries had changed it to the French . . . Montagne.

He was tempted to grab them from their honored place on the wall, to put on the mask, to bang the drum with one hand and shake the rattles with the other, to break the spell that chained Mike to the television set.

He looked at the figures on the screen.

"Do they look like any Indians we've ever known . . . do they? Do we talk like that?" Joey could no longer contain himself.

"They are *phony*. They are one big fake. Fake costumes, fake make-up, and worst of all . . . they're being used— like puppets, like clowns. Can't you see? They're not human. Everything they say, everything they do is funny, or supposed to be funny. It's not fair. It's just a bunch of commercial garbage. Does Papa Montagne look like that? Do you? Does Mom?" Joey's voice was angry. He was shouting loud enough to drown out the television voices.

TV VOICE: Why, Little Bull, if they discover oil on your property, you'll be rich. You'll be able to buy as much firewater as you like for the rest of your life.

LITTLE BULL: Me no likum firewater. Make skin red. Then me redskin, like you say. Me better buy tepee.

"I get it . . . I get it," Joey shouted, bolting from the room and Mike's presence.

The headache had magnified, tightening itself into a ring of pain around his head. Upstairs, he walked slowly into the bathroom and turned on the cold water. He held a hand towel under the faucet, soaking it well, then twisted it into a compress. He caught a glimpse of himself in the mirror and saw the effect of his anger on his face. Back in his bedroom, he raised the window shade, allowing the moonlight to substitute for the light of the lamp on the table near his bed. Placing the cold compress across his forehead, he lay back on the pillow, waiting for the cold towel to bring him even slight comfort. The room was dark and quiet, but only for a few seconds. The noise from the lower floor seeped through the walls, and the doors and windows. He tried to shut it out by changing his position, but each turn made him more uncomfortable. He guided his mind toward thoughts which could distract him. Concentrate. Think about something away from the pain and the noise.

—Why should I have to hide up here, nursing myself like

some wounded animal, while he sits down there fouling the room with his presence. He doesn't belong in a room like that, with his smell and his sweat. And what gives him the right to stake it off as his territory, to exclude me?

Joey thought about the many times in his childhood, when the living room was his favorite place to be, the times he would listen to Papa Montagne telling him strange stories before his bedtime, sending him off to dream about the people with false faces, or the sky dwellers. Or the holidays, like Christmas, when the room took on the beauty of the twinkling tree, sprouting with balls and candy canes and tinsel, and the huge, regal wreaths in the windows.

Now, it was Mike's room, and it no longer seemed to belong to the whole family.

Although the room was large, with high decorative ceilings common to the houses constructed in the 1850's, Lily Montagne had been successful in reducing its spacious dimensions, making it warm and comfortable.

The older Montagnes, Papa and Mama, had bought the house from its previous owners when they came to Brooklyn from Canada. The original furniture had the fine details and workmanship that only craftsmen could lavish on sofas, and tables, and chairs carefully carved by hand. In her desire to keep up with changing fashions, Mama Montagne eventually replaced the old pieces with assembly-line modern from nearby Abraham & Straus, and the department store furniture had occupied the house through the war years until her death.

When Big Joe brought Lily down from the reservation as his young bride to live with the Montagne family, she was delighted with the beauty and strength of the old house. When she discovered the abandoned, neglected

Victorian furniture in the basement, she asked Papa for permission to bring it out of the shadows and into the air and space above. Slowly, Lily transformed the room into the semblance of its former self, adding damask drapes, a large, impressive Persian rug for which she had bargained with a Lebanese merchant on Atlantic Avenue, and the twin petit point hassocks she found at an auction in the neighborhood.

Upstairs, she had done the same, bringing to each room, the bedrooms and the bathrooms, her ideas of furnishings to match the personalities of the men of the household—Papa, the Montagne brothers, Mike and Joe, and her young son.

Everything seemed right, to belong, in proper proportion—except for Mike, who trampled through the house and its rooms like some huge primordial creature, unmindful of the time and effort it had taken to give the family a quiet, comfortable place in which to live.

The year before, Mike had insisted on replacing the old black and white television console with a huge color set, which upset the harmony of the room. From that time on, it seemed to Joey, the room belonged to Mike, who took possession of it to witness the parade of television programs that marched across the screen every evening.

And Joey had come to appreciate the privacy of his own room, where he could shut himself away from the rest of the house. Like tonight.

His head felt lighter, liberated from the weight of the headache by the aspirin and the compress. His eyes were giving in to the need to sleep, and he drifted off into a white and silent vacuum.

A short time later he was awakened by a gentle tapping on the door and his mother's soft voice.

"Joey, Joey, are you all right?"

"I'm okay, Mom. Come in."

Lily Montagne walked to the night table and switched on the lamp. She picked up the compress which had fallen to the floor.

"Headache?"

"Right. A real lulu this time." Joey's voice was dry and harsh.

"Move over, Joey. Let me sit down." Lily sat on the side of the bed. "Joey, have you two been at it again?"

"Does it show?"

"Yes! Number one, you look lousy. Number two, it's Thursday night, and it's been happening every Thursday night since the program started. I wish there was a way I could keep you two from tearing each other apart. You should have come with me to the Le Bruns."

"Mom, this is my home too, isn't it? I would have gone out, gone somewhere, to the Neighborhood Center, but I had to rehearse my songs for tomorrow. You'd think the house is big enough, so that he couldn't bug me from down there. But he does it. He does it beautifully. Him and those programs of his. Playing that damn thing so loud I bet the mayor could hear it at City Hall. King Kong. Sitting there as though he were the only one in the world . . . him and those phony Indians."

"Joey, I wish you wouldn't talk that way. He's your uncle. He works hard and he's entitled to his enjoyment. After all, he bought the color television so we could all enjoy it, and you know how much Papa Montagne likes to watch it."

"Yeah, I know, Mom. But buying the television doesn't mean he's bought my respect. Doesn't he see what that program's doing? They're insulting us! It doesn't matter that those jerks are supposed to be Navajos. The whole program is just one big lie. It's some stupid Hollywood idea of the way Indians live. And it's probably being written by some smart son of a Hungarian immigrant, who has never been near a reservation, and probably writes the darn thing from his air-conditioned Park Avenue penthouse."

"Joey, they're not hurting anybody, are they? In fact, they're making a lot of people laugh. And these days, we need as many laughs as we can get."

Joey studied his mother's face. "Mom, *you* don't look like that."

"Like what, Joey?"

"Like those cheap, distorted clowns he watches down there."

"Am I supposed to?"

"No, Mom! That's the whole idea. We're Indian, but we don't look or act the way *they* do," he retorted, tossing his head sharply in the direction of the TV sounds.

"We're different, Joey. We've been living in New York a couple of generations. They're from out West."

"Why is it so hard to make you both understand? They're using a stereotype, Mom. The old Hollywood image of what Indians are like . . . and the whole country is watching and laughing and believing it. Don't you see? People accept that stupid program as the truth. They expect all Indians to look and act like *that*."

"You're taking it too seriously, Joey. Your uncle enjoys it and, from what I read in the papers, he isn't the only one. It's a very popular program. Should I apologize if—even I find it amusing?" Lily asked, smiling gently.

—What's the use, he thought. I really shouldn't take it out on her.

"Can I fix you a cup of tea?" Lily offered. "That always seems to help a little. Do you want me to bring it up to you?"

"No, that's okay, Mom. I'll come downstairs."

They walked into the hallway and down the stairs to the kitchen.

"Maybe it *is* louder than it should be," Lily thought as they passed the living room, "but how do you tell Mike anything?"

Joey sat at the kitchen table watching his mother rinse the kettle.

"Can I give you a bit of advice, Joey?"

"Be my guest, Mrs. Montagne."

"If you and Mike don't agree about something, try to understand that he's not perfect. None of us are. It's all right to disagree, but you should show him respect. Without him, I don't know where we'd be. I hate to see you two arguing so much lately. And I know Big Joe wouldn't have liked it either."

Joey recognized the truth in her words, but he hated it when she defended Mike by using his father's name. If Big Joe Montagne were still alive, there probably would be no arguments with Mike. Maybe he'd have been more of a friend, not an uncle posing as a father. Sometimes Joey felt that Mike, in some strange distortion of the truth, was blaming them all for Big Joe's death.

The hissing kettle brought Joey out of his thoughts. Lily, who hated insipid teabags and the weak brew they created, poured three spoonfuls of imported British tea into the kettle to boil and steep.

Joey asked about her visit to the Le Bruns. "How is the old lady?"

"For a woman of eighty-two, I'd say she's in pretty good shape, but she has that bad feeling about dying here in Brooklyn. She wants to go back to Caughnawaga, but the Le Bruns can't do that now. They have no one to take care of her up there, and Marguerite doesn't know what they can do."

"How come Papa doesn't feel that way?" Joey asked.

"Maybe he does, Joey, even if he doesn't say so, but it's different for a woman. Your grandfather feels that so much of his body and soul belong to the city. He's given it the best years of his life. Sometimes I think that he feels the city will crumble to dust if he leaves his precious buildings and bridges."

"Mom, aren't you exaggerating?"

"Maybe, but only a little, Joey. The Le Bruns just don't feel the same about New York as your uncle and your grandfather do. As Big Joe did."

"Mom, do you realize how much we mention Big Joe lately?"

"Yes, I do, Joey."

"Why, Mom?"

"He's always with us, Joey. Maybe now, more than ever."

"I think it's because we need him. It's like by saying his name often there's a chance that he'll come back . . . that it didn't happen."

"We know that's not possible, Joey."

"I know, Mom."

Lily's eyes clouded over. It seemed to happen no matter how often she sat with her son and talked about the man they both had loved and lost.

"Hey, here you are trying to help me get over my lousy headache, and I go giving you the blues."

"No, Joey. It's good to talk about Big Joe. That's the wonderful thing about my life with him. He gave me so much that was good, made my life a better one by becoming a part of me. I'll never lose him. But the saddest thing is that he's not here to see what a fine son you are, and that he can't enjoy you as I do. You know, Joey, you are so much like him . . . your looks, your walk. Sometimes, that upsets me."

Joey hesitated, looking at his hands nervously. "Mom, have you ever thought of marrying again?"

"Yes, Joey. I've thought about it. But somehow, I don't want to. Maybe . . . if someday . . . Joey, do you know that your uncle Mike has asked me?"

"No, I didn't, Mom."

—Now, he even wants her. It's not enough that he runs the whole show around here. He wants my mother, too.

Seeing the hurt expression on Joey's face, Lily quickly added, "Mike's not for me. Not after a man as good and gentle as your father was. I feel sorry for Mike, that he's never settled down with a woman. But that's no reason for marrying him."

"Mom, listen to me." Joey reached for Lily's hand. "If you ever meet someone, you do whatever you feel like doing, and don't worry about me. I know one thing. Big Joe would want you to be happy."

"In my own way, I'm doing all right, Joey. I've got you three men to look after, and that keeps me busy. You know I love to cook and bake, and to shop and entertain. And this house is a beautiful one to live in. I've seen you grow up, and I've watched Papa grow older. I've been able to shut out the troubles of the world. I just hope you Montagnes will keep the house until you're good and tired of it. Like maybe never."

She poured the two cups of tea, and they slowly sipped the fragrant liquid, and knew that their conversation had brought them to a deeper understanding.

"Joey, I'm going inside to watch. Don't stay up too late. You've got a big day tomorrow."

"Ree-ee-lly big." Joey mimicked Ed Sullivan.

He followed Lily from the kitchen to the hallway, stopping to grab a sweater from the closet beneath the stairs.

She walked into the living room, closing the doors behind her. In a few seconds her tinkling laughter had joined with Mike's.

Joey bolted blindly upstairs to the third floor and the door that led to the roof.

2

THE ROOF was always quiet and dark and cool, and Joey knew that in the darkness he could collect his thoughts and arrange them neatly from the shambles Mike had made of them. He gazed out over the edge of the roof. The orderly pattern of buildings and streets, and the smooth line of traffic on the Gowanus Expressway seemed to restore his calm.

He loved the roof because it seemed to place him in the center of the city, even though it was hidden away among the tenements and factory lofts. Looking in any direction, he felt like some proud spider sitting in the heart of its lacy web, studying its handiwork. He admired the gossamer angles and curves, the patterns of glass and steel—the infinite reflections of light that were Manhattan at night.

His mind leaped to other places and other times—the pyramids in Egypt, the lost city of Machu Picchu high in the Andes, the lofty spires of Chartres—places where man had conquered time and space to leave traces of his genius. New York, at night, with its fingers of light scraping at the heavens, belonged to this century. How long would it endure?

—My grandfather and my father and Mike, and hundreds of men like them, mixed their muscle and sweat with steel to make many of those buildings and bridges, Joey thought. Do they love New York the way I do? Is their job just a job to them? Does their pride get lost somewhere between the blueprints and the topping off? When they are on the ground, walking through the city streets, do they have any urge to shout to everybody near them . . . that's mine, I did it, without me it would not be there?

Joey thought of his own pride in the beauty the Montagnes had given the city. At times, he felt a deep need to tell people that the buildings they took for granted were born at a terrible price. But the thought remained buried, where only he could know it.

—Could I ever have gone up there with them, and made of my life what they have of theirs? Would they have lent me their strength, their power to push and pull an architect's dream until it took the shape of reality?

Those questions had nagged at Joey for the many weeks since he had made his decision to apply for the Ironworkers' Union scholarship that would give him the chance to continue his education. He would be breaking the chain that led from Papa to Big Joe to Mike. High steel was not for him, and never would be, and that knowledge had made him feel like a deserter. But he had made his decision. Mike would be the last of the Montagnes to work up there.

He turned to look in the direction of the East River. Although it was obscured from his vision, Joey knew that the

United Nations Secretariat rose out of the darkness there, lighting the night sky with floor after floor of beauty.

—That building belongs to me. It's mine because it cost my father his life. I don't know if anyone will ever understand that. And each time I pass it, or see it in a book or magazine, it reminds me that it took my father from me, that he fell to his death. He never saw it as it looks now.

The noise of the city was muffled, and Joey watched the semaphore pattern of traffic—the blinking reds in one direction, the oncoming whites in the other. A sadness seemed to envelop the scene. In his mind the Secretariat became a monument to his father.

—What do other fathers leave to their sons? Did some Egyptian boy stand in the shadow of the pyramids and think what I am thinking? Did some young Inca warrior feel the same about the temple hidden in the Andean mist? Did the son of some medieval French stonecutter claim Chartres as his very own? Had those boys laughed in triumph, had they feasted and fallen drunk in celebration? Or had they wept too, as he had, because the building of a tomb, a temple, a cathedral had cost their fathers' lives?

A jumbled image of his father took shape in his memory. It seemed so long ago, since that day when he was five, that the Montagnes, dressed in black, had gone to Caughnawaga to bury Big Joe.

Joey had never been content to live with only a few faded photographs and the stories he'd heard the men in the neighborhood tell about the legendary strength and warmth of Big Joe.

People who had worked with his father always told Joey how much he looked like Big Joe, when he'd been in his teens. To many of Joey's friends and relatives, it seemed as though all the Montagne men had been poured from some marvelous Mohawk mold. Yet, those who knew them well were aware of how different the Montagne brothers, Big Joe and Mike, were. Although they looked alike, and yet different, in the mysterious way that brothers growing up in the same household could be, the Montagne boys both left strong impressions on anyone they met. Nearly six feet tall, finely proportioned and muscular, they looked even taller because of their natural, erect posture. Either of them could have easily provided a sculptor with the classic proportions for the perfect Mohawk. Broad foreheads framed in black hair, aquiline noses, full lips covering porcelain teeth, and square, jutting chins. Yet, what most people noticed were the deep, brown-black penetrating eyes, protected by thick, long, black lashes. Perhaps it was the eyes that made the difference. Mike's seemed distant at times, as though they mirrored the questions about his life that he had not yet answered, while Big Joe's had been warm and friendly, and seemed to say that he had found much happiness with his lovely wife and fine baby boy.

Whereas Big Joe tackled life with a sense of calm and assurance and with a gentleness that he seemed to lend to all those around him, Mike was all bluster and bragging, sound and fury. Mike worshipped his older brother but seemed to feel that he somehow had to make up for Big Joe's modesty by arguing and fighting with anyone who doubted that the Montagnes were the best ironworkers in the business.

Joey once heard his grandfather tell some of his relatives, "Why, Big Joe could probably do anything he'd like to with his life, even without an education. But Mike—he's different. It's like he's got hot iron flowing through his veins, pouring into his brain, pushing him to be the best ironworker in the world. With him, his work is like a curse. The white man took everything else away from our people—our land, our pride, our way of life—but somehow, we Indians made our way into ironwork, and Mike's going to stay on top, where no Irish or Italian or any of them can take his place. We've got something the white man can't take away."

When Papa Montagne retired, the whole neighborhood knew that his sons, and their sons after them, would make sure that ironwork and the Montagne name would stay linked together like natural elements.

Now, Mike was the only Montagne left in ironwork and his plans for Joey's future were bolted into place, solid and immovable. Joey would take Big Joe's place. By joining Mike's work crew, Joey could assure the Montagne name its fame once more. So sure was Mike that this would happen that he never spoke to anyone about it, never asking Lily, who had lost her husband to high steel, how she might feel about Joey joining up with him.

And Mike saw no need to talk with Joey about his future. Had Papa ever asked his sons if they had any ideas about how they were to earn their living? If ironwork was good enough for the father, it could be a fine way of life for his strong, healthy sons. No questions. When they graduated from high school they went through the Union's apprentice program. And they were not surprised to meet many other Mohawk fathers registering their sons. Any of the boys with strange ideas of becoming lawyers or salesmen or of leaving to join the Army bent quietly and quickly to their fathers' wills. And the Mohawk women watched as their sons joined their husbands. They tried to bury their fears and ignore their bad dreams about the accidents and danger that their sons would face.

Lily learned to live with the reality that the men around her—Big Joe, Mike, and Papa—had chosen a way of life that seemed to suit their ruggedness, their size and strength. And as she watched Joey grow, she wondered if he, too, would be claimed by high steel, by the fever of the Montagne men to be the best of the Mohawk ironworkers. In Joey she saw a reflection of her own gentleness, and she secretly hoped that he would find a way that would lead him far from the danger the other Montagnes seemed to thrive on.

Joey thought about the gentle people in the world. Were they always fated to be pushed around by the Mikes? Had Mike always been rough and crude and loud? What private demons had lodged themselves in his soul, blinding him to the knowledge that he was a bully, plundering his roughshod way into others' lives, robbing them of the freedom to plan their own destinies? Joey frowned, wondering how Mike would finally accept the news when he was told that Joey had decided not to follow in the Montagne mold—that he was going to try his hand at becoming an actor instead of a human fly, swapping steel for the stage.

The headache had faded, and Joey knew that the few quiet moments on the roof and the awesome beauty of the city had done much to restore his faith in himself.

He took a deep breath of the night air, feeling more ready for tomorrow than he had for weeks. There had been too many days and nights of hard work to let Mike ruin it all. Joey no longer questioned the wisdom of his decision to try out for Plays and Players, the dramatic group at school. He might as well find out whether or not he could face an audience, playing a major part in a musical.

The metal doorway of the roof squeaked open.

"I knew you'd be here." Birdie rushed into Joey's embrace and kissed him lightly; she glowed with an inner excitement. Behind her walked Papa Montagne, breathing heavily from the climb to the rooftop.

"How did the interviews go today?" Joey asked.

"Just great, Joey," she said. "I wish Mr. Marshall had been there. I'd have given him the greatest kiss ever for getting me started on the idea. And as for Papa here, once I explained what it was that I was doing, he was absolutely groovy."

"What does groovy mean, Birdie? If it means that I was very pleased that someone is taking the trouble to listen to our old stories and songs, then I guess I was . . . what did you say? . . . groovy," Papa offered.

"Joey," Birdie went on in a smiling, breathless way. "I sat Papa down at the table with the tape recorder, and in a few minutes, he was talking into it like an old pro. For a little while, he described the reservation as he remembered it when he was a kid, and we went through the seasons, you know, what they did in the spring, and then the harvest, and the winter. He sang an old harvest song, and a river song that the canoers used to sing on the way to the fur market. He was wonderful. The songs were absolutely beautiful. Then to top it all off, he told of visiting a longhouse for a False Face ceremony. It was creepy, Joey—naturally, marvelously creepy. I got goosepimples."

"I hope you know, Papa, that you are the first contributor to Birdie Le Brun's 'Oral History of the Caughna-wagas,' " Joey told the old man.

"I don't really know what that means either, Joey. You kids speak fancy language these days. Different from us old people. If you mean that I spent some time with a pretty young woman, while she listened to a creaky old man talk and sing—and by the way, Birdie, I enjoyed myself very much—if that's what you mean, I'll do it again any time she invites me."

Birdie hugged the old man tightly. "Papa, you're too much! I can't imagine a time when you're not going to be with us."

"This old timer doesn't expect to go yet. Not if you still need me," Papa Montagne said.

"We need you, Papa. We'll always need you." Birdie's voice caught in her throat.

"Well, I think that's good, that you young people don't forget us old ones. We're not of much use to anybody, crawling through our last days. But we do have the stories and the songs, if anyone wants to listen."

"We need to listen, Papa," Joey said. "They're important to us too."

The old man leaned against the doorway. "How the world changes! When I was a boy, I sang and danced with the trees and the river as my witnesses. Now, I sit in front of a funny little machine, and sing and talk while the little wheels go around. Then Birdie pushes a button and my voice comes back to me, and even though I sang low, it comes back strong and clear. I am sure I disturb all the others in the room."

"But, Papa, you didn't disturb anyone. Didn't you notice

how quiet everyone got? They all stopped what they were doing to listen," Birdie assured him.

"Yes, I saw that. And it made me nervous. I am not a singer, or a teller of stories. There are other old ones who do it better than me. Give me my beams to walk on, or my rivets to toss. There was a Montagne once, who could sing and dance with the best of them. My brother Albert. He's the one who should be here to sing for your machine." His voice faded to a mumble.

"What's that, Papa?" Joey asked.

"If you think you can sing, Joey, you should have heard my brother Albert, the one who thought I was crazy to go into ironwork. The one I thought was crazy to join up with the circus in Montreal. So many years ago. You never knew about him, Joey. He was called the family disgrace because he left the reservation to join a white man's circus. 'Imagine,' they said, 'one of the Montagnes dressed in paint and feathers singing and dancing like a madman for the white man's amusement.' But he was not so mad, that Albert. He traveled all over the world, telling people about Indians. He was famous. Why, I even took the longest train ride of my life from Montreal to New York to see him perform at the Palace. He introduced me to Sophie Tucker, who was then a handsome young woman. 'Sophie,' he said, 'this is my brother Joseph, who hangs from bridges by his teeth!' We all laughed together, the blonde white woman, the painted Mohawk, and the boomer from Montreal."

Joey had never heard Papa talk about his brother, and he was grateful to the old man for telling them about a Montagne who had not answered the call of high steel. Suddenly, he felt a strange kinship to Albert, who offered himself to the circus as a performer, who would sing and dance his way into the memory of his audiences, who must have been quite a vision riding into the arena in the full regalia of a Mohawk warrior. A real Indian, doing real Indian things—not like the phonies that would follow him, in the movies and on television.

"Papa, will you tell us more about Albert, for the tape recorder?" Birdie asked.

"Why not, Birdie? I will tell you anything you want to hear before these lips make no more sense at all. And now, young ones, I feel the chill of the night air. A cup of Lily's tea is what I need. Good night." He walked slowly to the door of the roof, and Joey and Birdie watched as his frail body drew itself to a noble height, framed in the sudden light coming from the door.

Birdie and Joey stood there, arm in arm, gazing at the arrows of red and white lights which flowed out through the streets and highways. The stars, struggling to show themselves through the curtain of haze, blinked here and there, silent witnesses of the meeting taking place on the Brooklyn roof.

"Joey, I hate to bring it up again, but have you told Mike about your plans?"

"No, I haven't told him yet."

"What are you waiting for, Joey? You only have a couple of days to get the application in, you know."

"I was going to tell him tonight, but it would take a ton of dynamite to blast him away from that TV set. I guess I'll have to wait until after the performance tomorrow night. I don't know if I can handle Mike and opening night jitters at the same time," he said.

"You know best, Joey. I don't think I'll ever have your patience. I would have flipped my lid long ago."

"Maybe. It's different when you live with Mike. I don't want him taking it out on Mom or Papa. When he gets a mad on, it takes a good long time for it to leave him."

"You ought to tell me to mind my own business," Birdie apologized.

Joey took her face in his hands, and his eyes echoed his smile.

"Okay, mind your own business."

"But my business is your business," they told each other simultaneously.

Laughing and filled with the pleasure that their minds had caught the same idea at the same moment, they kissed and walked slowly from the edge of the roof to the door. They enjoyed the warmth and comfort they felt in each other's presence. The bonds that tied their families together had allowed them to share many of their childhood experiences, and they were not surprised to watch platonic feelings give way to emotions they could not define, but rather accept as instinctive and natural. They needed each other, and their affection had grown into love.

Downstairs, they passed the living room where Mike still sat watching another program. His laughter echoed through the house, silenced finally when Joey slammed the front door to the street.

"You don't have to walk me home, Joey."

"I know, but I want to."

As they walked from Schermerhorn to the house where the Le Bruns lived, they realized how different the city was from the ground. The air was heavy with the industrial fumes, and garbage cans stood full and neglected, waiting for the morning trucks.

As they looked up at the houses they were passing, they

could see the glow of television tubes flickering through curtains and window shades. Joey shuddered when he thought how many people in them had been watching "Wild Woolly West."

Birdie was glad they were away from Mike, and the sense of suffocation he seemed to bring to anybody who interrupted him as he watched his programs.

"You know, Joey, Mr. Marshall asked the class for a definition of 'gross' today. He said he thought we were abusing it, that he was tired of hearing it. And you know what I was tempted to tell him? Gross means Mike. Mike really means gross."

"I can think of lots of other words to describe Mike."

"But he *is* gross. Absolutely, definitely gross," Birdie repeated.

"Do you want a dozen others? I can rattle them off in less than a minute."

"Oh, let's stop talking about him. Why spoil a good night's sleep?"

They had reached Birdie's house. Joey kissed her on the cheek.

"Sleep well," he told her as she paused at the door.

"You, too. You've got to knock them dead tomorrow night, Joey. Take it easy and don't let him get you down."

"I won't. By the way, I'll pick you up at about six. Okay?"

"That's fine."

Joey watched the door close behind her.

3

THE PLAYS AND PLAYERS had had a difficult time deciding
on their musical performance for the season. For weeks
they read and discussed the many possibilities, and the
problems involved in each. *The Music Man* would need
a large cast, and young children would have to be brought
in from elementary and junior high schools, so it was discarded. The Rodgers and Hammerstein musicals had been
done too many times by neighboring schools. "West Side
Story" was a popular choice with the group's officers but
was abandoned because there would never be enough
dance talent which the play required. Finally, they chose
to do *The Fantasticks*. It was a simple musical, with a
small cast, lovely songs which had flooded radio and television programs for months, and a strong message for a
young audience. The two youngsters who were the leads
defied their parents, and set out to see the world and learn
about human nature, firsthand. Their adventures were
filled with moments of comedy, and many more that were
touching and romantic, and the score complemented the

action beautifully with many songs that told of the marvel of being alive.

Joey was thrilled when he reached the final audition and won the important part of El Gallo, a combination narrator-adventurer, who would conduct the youngsters from the small garden that separated their homes to the exciting cities that awaited them outside.

The many weeks of rehearsal flowed smoothly by, and in the days before the opening, the pieces began to fit together like a vast, jigsaw puzzle made up of set designs and construction, costumes, the intricate lighting, and the performances.

The stage at the high school was well endowed with all of the paraphernalia that would allow any amateur performer to work with a fine semblance of the professional. The lighting board could offer the designer a dozen or more variations, ranging from a pinpoint of light on an actor's face to flooding the entire stage. Scenery could be flown—that is, hauled up out of sight against the stage ceiling—and, in recent years, a cyclorama and scrim curtain had been installed to add special effects fine enough to rival those of any Broadway stage.

The problem in staging *The Fantasticks* was to discover and keep its elusive quality of intimacy and its delicate use of whimsy and charm. Jim Marshall, the faculty advisor, knew the production could get lost on the large stage if it were not whittled down to a small segment of its size. Consulting with the students who had designed and built the simple setting of small gardens on each side of a brick wall running down the center, he had guided them toward successfully achieving the effect they sought. The audience would not be allowed to let its eyes wander from the small central arena where love and piracy and adventure—the sadness and exuberance of youth—would soon light up the stage.

When Joey and Birdie arrived, the small combo of piano, bass, and drums was already rehearsing. As they walked down the center aisle of the echoing auditorium, they could hear Jim Marshall shouting some of the lighting cues for the second act.

Suddenly, the stage was bathed in a delicate blue which gradually changed into the deep purple of a summer evening. The stagehands were busy checking the final placement of the set on the stage floor. Miss Hopkins, looking like a comic-book version of Mother Nature, puffed out the colorful crepe paper flowers and vegetables in an effort to make them look as real as possible. Rotund and red-cheeked, she couldn't help but look pleasant. People meeting her for the first time knew, almost instinctively, that she was head of the Home Economics department.

She noticed Joey and Birdie standing transfixed in the aisle.

"Good evening, people," she greeted them warmly. Her large hands were buried in an artificial eggplant, which she carefully puffed to its full size.

"Hi, Miss Hopkins. Gee, they look absolutely good enough to eat," Joey responded.

"Well, you know, kids, when I was your age we were taught, in that famous poem, that only God could make a tree. I'm not so sure about that anymore. Give our art department some crepe paper and glue and scissors and their busy little fingers do a pretty good job. I just told Mr. Marshall I'd give them the onceover to see that they looked convincing enough from the first few rows."

"They do, Miss Hopkins," Birdie told her.

"You know something, Birdie, I don't think it really matters. This is such a marvelous production that the audience will never notice these old vegetables anyway. Why, take this rose. It's almost as big as I am." She pointed to a large pink and purple cabbage rose. "Well, not really. Nothing could be that big." Her Santa laugh filled the stage area.

"Miss Hopkins, all kidding aside, I think your girls have done a terrific job with the costumes. You know, we get so darned busy doing our own little thing, we take some things for granted," said Joey.

"Why, that's very nice of you to say so, Joey. And at the risk of sounding like president of the Mutual Admiration Society, I'd like to tell you how absolutely splendid I think you are, young man. All of you kids have really sunk your hearts and souls into what you're doing, and it shows." She noticed Joey blushing. "And I'm not just blowing hot air. But you especially, Joey. I think it's grand the way you've captured the character of El Gallo. Why, you're so mischievously likeable up there, you could kidnap me anytime . . . that is, if you think you could manage to carry me away. And when you start to sing 'Try to Remember' I get goosebumps all over, about the size of a quarter. I don't know what it is young man, but you've got something."

"Thanks, Miss Hopkins. That's very good to hear." Joey smiled.

She had bent over to freshen up a huge squash. "There. How does that look? I guess that's the last of them."

"Delicious," Birdie answered.

"Oh, oh . . . don't just stand there. Don't you know when

an old lady has to be helped up. Talk about the leaning tower of Pisa."

Joey offered her his hand and helped her to straighten.

She caught her breath. "If either of you ever get to where you enjoy life as much as I do, try to keep it from showing," she advised, smoothing out her dress, and bringing the belt around to the front.

Joey enjoyed the way Miss Hopkins made fun of her girth, and looking at her, wondered how old she really was. Through all of his years at school, he had found it diffi-cut to guess the age of many of his teachers. He knew Mr. Marshall was in his early forties, because during an English class he had told them about his childhood and his World War II experiences, making no secret of his age. With women teachers, it was harder to judge. They had the benefit of cosmetics, and hair coloring, and their fashions changed so much more frequently than the male teachers. He guessed Miss Hopkins to be about fifty-five or fifty-seven, and then dismissed the thought of her numerical age entirely. Her spirit made her one of the most popular teachers at school, and she related warmly to young people and their problems.

"Are you nervous, Joey?" she asked.

"What do you think, Miss Hopkins? Does it show that bad?"

"Not at all, Joey." She patted his arm. "You look as cool as that luscious cucumber, if you'll pardon the cliché. I know you're going to be a knockout tonight, and so are the others. I think it's remarkable how wonderfully you've all caught the spirit of the play. You've made it a really lovely thing, and it shows every minute, in the way you all look and sound up there."

Joey was about to thank her for her encouragement when he heard Mr. Marshall shouting for him from the catwalk, high above the stage.

"Joey! Joey Montagne, is that you? Up here!" His voice sounded faint and distant, coming from where he stood, about forty feet in the flies. "I want to try the confetti bit. Let me know how it looks."

"Okay," Joey shouted back.

At various times during the action, the character known as the Mute had to drift across the stage carrying various papier-mâché props, like a huge smiling sun or a wistful full moon. The most effective of his props were handfuls of confetti which he tossed capriciously into the air to represent at different moments, sunshine, falling leaves, moonbeams, or the simple joy experienced by the characters. During rehearsal, doing it from the actual stage floor, Marshall thought that it looked too earthbound, that the whole effect needed to be lifted and given the semblance of coming from the sky. To do this, he decided to add more confetti drifting from the area above the stage.

Slowly, the bits of colored paper fluttered downward, catching in the light like small bits of rainbow.

"Mr. Marshall . . . that's breathtaking!" shouted Miss Hopkins.

"It's terrific, Mr. Marshall!" Joey exclaimed.

Chuck Smith, the prop boy, who would be doing it during the performance, couldn't restrain his approval. "That's the best thing that happens all night, Mr. Marshall. And just think—*I'm* doing it!"

They all laughed. Chuck was anxious to try it himself, but he was busy fastening the scenery.

"Joey, do me a favor, will you?" Marshall asked.

"Sure."

"You know how to get up here—the staircase out there in the hall. Come on up. I'd like to see how it looks from down there."

"Oh, no!" Joey muttered to himself.

He had watched the stage crew prancing back and forth on the catwalk above, suspended on heavy chains from the ceiling, and it always made him nervous. Big Joe falling. Big Joe dead. He knew he had kept his dislike of open height from Mr. Marshall, and this was not the time to let it reveal itself.

He passed Mr. Marshall coming down the stairs.

"You all right, kid?" Jim Marshall asked. He thought Joey looked worried.

"I'm okay."

"You keep looking like that, and you'll have me worried. Want a pass to the nurse's office?"

"Very fun-ny! Seriously though, I'm okay. Just a bad case of opening night willies." He had often read that even the most polished performers had their private rituals for overcoming the jitters that came in the first few minutes after the curtain's rise. For Joey, that knowledge was small consolation and he began to wonder if the trip into the flies would only compound the queasy feeling in his stomach.

In a few moments he had opened the door to the catwalk. He was glad it was dark. He could grope his way across to the center, holding onto the cable, without anyone knowing how slowly and cautiously he was moving. What if he were to freeze?

"No, please . . . no!" an inner voice whispered weakly.

His palms were cold and sweaty, and he listened to the

magnified sound of his heart pounding away with each step.

The large paper bag of confetti was lying in the center of the walk so that it could be thrown down in either direction, left or right.

"Joey, you up there?" Marshall shouted from below.

"Just a minute. It's so darn dark up here. I—I—I—how—how's this?" he stammered, hating himself.

As he bent to grab a handful, the catwalk swayed slightly.

"Do it! Get it over with and get down!" his mind prompted desperately.

The vertigo had begun. He could feel his dinner coming up into his chest. Curling one hand around his throat hoping it wouldn't happen, he closed his eyes and with his free hand he scooped into the bag. Some of the confetti stuck to his damp hands.

Slowly, it drifted to the stage floor.

"Magnificent! If I do say so myself," Marshall shouted. "Okay, come on down now, Joey. Time to get going with the grease paint."

Joey never really knew how he made it down to the safety of the dressing room. Each agonizing inch seemed to heighten the uncomfortable sensations in his stomach. With his eyes almost closed, he felt the rush of air as he opened the door to the stairway. He wiped his hands on his trousers, and hoped his face would not reveal his reaction to the climb on the catwalk. As he walked downstairs, the bad feeling began to subside.

"Funny," his mind told him, "you never get sick up on your roof. What is it with you?"

And he was able to answer himself. "The roof is solid.

It's anchored to the ground. Firm. Solid. It's the open space that does it. A catwalk. A scaffold. Walking . . . walking the beams . . . like Mike and Papa and Big Joe. Suddenly, the ominous echo repeated itself. Big Joe falling. Big Joe dead.

His thoughts were dispelled by the noises in the backstage area. In the dressing room, where Birdie was helping one of the actors with graying of his hair, Joey was glad for the excited conversation that surrounded him.

"Looks like standing room only, Joey," said Ken Friedman, who was playing one of the fathers. "They sure must be gluttons for punishment."

"Not at all, young man," Joey told him with mock Shakespearean solemnity. "You can rest assured that this band of culture vultures will be witnessing a theatrical experience, second to none."

"Wow, mister, are you sure?" Ken answered. "'Cause it isn't every day that they pay three bucks for something that isn't bowling or a movie."

"Sirrah, I charge you to give them the performance of your life. They must leave this building with memories to last them a lifetime," Joey replied.

"Yeah, but what'll I say to them when they come to my register at the supermarket next week? Just think, Joey, a star one night, a clerk the next."

"Never, Sir Friedman," Joey admonished in his most Olivier tone. "Once a star, always a star."

They all laughed, yet beneath the laughter they could each detect their impatience to see the evening begin, to hear the first clatter of applause. Ken was examining his image in the mirror and seemed pleased with the transformation Birdie had helped to bring about.

"Next?" Birdie announced.

Joey took the chair that Ken had just left. Birdie dipped her hands into a large jar of bronze grease paint. As she gentle massaged the makeup into his skin, spreading it evenly around his face and neck, Joey felt as though her assurance and calm were flowing into his body. The nervousness was disappearing, replaced by a growing sense of excitement.

It had seemed like only minutes since he'd arrived. Soon he was standing in the wings listening to the expectant audience and its busy noise of chatter and greeting as everyone settled into their seats. He squinted through a tiny tear in the maroon velvet curtain and discovered his mother, Mike, and Papa making their way down the aisle. Lily was smiling, unable to hide her excitement. Mike had stopped to talk to the Le Bruns.

Birdie had asked Mr. Marshall for permission to watch from the wings and he was delighted to grant it, feeling that her presence there would lend encouragement to Joey.

In rapid succession, the house lights dimmed and the overture began. The actors were in their places in the wings. The curtains slowly parted and the Mute made his way gracefully across the stage carrying the huge sun. Slowly, he lifted the large golden circle, and the stage was flooded with amber and pink and orange lights and shadows.

"Break a leg," Joey heard Birdie whisper. He checked the jauntiness of his large black hat, and flung his cape over one shoulder. Gracefully, with sure steps, he walked into the sunlight, and as he made his way across the stage, he felt in his heart that a new day had really begun.

Joey's voice, strong yet sweet enough, offered the audience an invitation to follow him into the lives of the boy and girl on stage, and into their own memories of young and innocent love.

He heard the applause, and then shut out the reality of the audience and the auditorium, taking on the swaggering countenance of El Gallo in the make-believe world of the play.

The moments flew, with entrances and exits, and Joey and the other performers knew the satisfaction accorded actors when the audience bathes them in waves of warm applause. More applause and cheering. *The Fantasticks* had worked its special magic, and the cast and the audience were glad to have shared its beauty.

4

WHILE THE AUDITORIUM was emptying, a number of people gathered in small groups, friends or relatives of the performers, eager to make their way backstage to offer praise and comments about the exciting production.

The cast, in the first few moments after the final bows, stood in the center of the stage. The lighting, no longer keyed to the special atmosphere of the little world Jim Marshall had created, showed their perspiration and fatigue. They knew their work was done, and from the generous applause and a number of vigorous "Bravos!," they had felt the audience's sincere appreciation.

Mr. Marshall was shouting from somewhere backstage. "Okay, kids. Open the curtains. Get ready, everybody, here they come." He walked to the small circle of performers and was lost in a sea of flailing arms and handshakes.

The curtains had been pulled to the sides of the stage, and the small bands of visitors made their way to where the actors were standing. The vast, echoing stage area was suddenly filled with the babble of happy chatter.

Joey saw Mike, Lily, and his grandfather and a number of their neighbors making their way across the stage.

Ken Friedman was surrounded by a large delegation of his family. A distinguished gray-haired man, whom Joey took to be Ken's grandfather, was telling Ken, "An actor. That's all this family needs is an actor. We haven't got enough troubles. And a regular Menasha Skulnik yet."

"A what?" Ken asked the old man.

"A Skulnik. A Skulnik," his grandfather repeated. "How could you be such a smart boy and not know what a Skulnik is?"

"So, Morris, don't confuse the boy. Tell him who Skulnik is," said a tall, well-dressed woman standing at his side.

"Skulnik is a performer so natural that he needs just to lift an eyebrow to make his audience laugh. He walks funny, he sings funny, he talks funny. You get my point?"

"You mean I was that good?" Ken asked.

"Not exactly *that* good. But for a beginner, not bad either." He turned to Joey. "But you, young man, were wonderful. I don't give compliments so easy. You acted perfect, and you sang sweet as honey. It was a pleasure to watch you."

"Thank you very much," Joey responded, touched by the man's sincerity.

Out of the noise and clamor came the delegation of Caughnawagas who had come to see Big Joe's boy perform. Lily, her arm linked to Papa Montagne's, was the first to reach her son.

"I loved it, Joey, and I really don't know what else to say. I shouldn't be surprised and yet I am." She seemed flustered and looked to Mike to help her find the words she wished to offer her son. Mike stood there silent.

Papa Montagne put his arm around his grandson's shoulder. "I'm proud of you, Joey." He glared at Mike. "We all are."

His words broke the obvious tension, and suddenly Joey was being slapped on the back and grabbed by the hands in a crush of congratulation.

"Great, Joey, just great!"

"You were a gas, kid!"

"That Frank Sinatra better watch it. Here comes Joey Montagne."

"Quiet, everybody," shouted Billy Le Brun, Birdie's older brother. "Let the guy say a few words."

Joey looked at the animated faces around him. One face, a mask that seemed annoyed, almost angry, stood out. Joey remembered last night, when Mike had shouted at him for standing in the living room like a dummy.

—Say something, you jerk. At least, something. Say it stank, or say you hated it. Just don't stand there as though I don't matter. Joey's thoughts spun in his head. —You can sit in our living room and rave your fool head off about those phony Indian clowns, and now suddenly you've lost your tongue. Blast you and your silence.

He realized the others were waiting for him to say something, and watching their smiling faces, he felt his anger slowly leaving him.

"Thanks, everybody, for coming tonight. If you enjoyed what you saw, we're really glad. It made me feel great to have you all out there rooting for me. And you know something, I could almost actually feel it—physically, I mean. I couldn't see you while I was up there . . . the audience is sort of like lost in the dark . . . but when you laughed or applauded, and even sometimes when you were silent, something reaches across from you to us. It seems to jump over that empty space between the first row and the stage, like some warm wave of friendship. It was weird and wonderful. And I want to thank you all."

"You must be beat, Joey," said Billy Le Brun. "I'll take walking on beams any day. You'll never get me up in front of people, singing and dancing, and saying all those fancy words. That takes guts."

"I don't know about that, Billy. I guess it takes a different kind of guts."

"Hey," Birdie interrupted, "you guys are in a rut with this 'guts' thing. I think Billy enjoys what he's doing, and Joey is happy when he's up there onstage. Isn't that what it's all about?"

"Leave it to my sister to tell us off. Boy, she's got guts." Billy smiled.

"Billy, baby, you know I love words, either speaking them or writing them. That's what makes me happy. So you see, how easy it is. Just find out what you like to do, and then go and do it. Now why don't you guys give Joey a chance to get all the junk off his face and change his clothes. We'll see you later."

"Good idea," said Billy.

Joey was slapped on the back at least a dozen times.

"So long, kid. See you later."

"Take it easy, Joey."

"Good night."

The group sauntered across the stage, except for the Montagnes and Birdie.

Birdie turned to Mike. "Well, Mike, what did you think of your nephew?"

"What am I supposed to say?"

"You're not *supposed* to say anything."

"You keep on fishin' for compliments, you and him. If he had a good time, I'm glad it's out of his system. He knows what I think of actors. A bunch of painted-up fags."

Joey couldn't hold back any longer. "What a big bag of contradictions you are. How come you don't think those jerks on 'Wild Woolly West' are . . . oh well, why should I waste my time."

"That's what I keep tellin' you. You're wastin' your time. And don't keep knockin' them TV actors. They aren't snot-nosed kids ready to graduate from high school. Actin' like jerks is their business. Most of them are a bunch of bums anyway, boozin' it up and runnin' around with dames. That's no kinda' life for you. You wanna' be one of them? I can't see it. And I know Big Joe wouldn't like it either."

"How do you know what Big Joe would like for his boy?" Papa said.

Lily was looking at the floor, trying to hide the hurt she was feeling. "Mike, Joey. Please drop it. It's been one of the nicest nights of my life. Please don't spoil it."

Jim Marshall came toward them from the wings with a man Joey had never seen before.

"Hello, Mrs. Montagne. You've got quite a boy here. I'm sure you don't need me to tell you that. By the way, I'd like you to meet a very good friend of mine. Hal Golding, meet the Montagnes."

Golding reminded Joey instantly of Yul Brynner. His strong face was made to look even more so by his shaved head. He was dressed in a casual, sporty style, looking like a strange combination of a Turkish wrestler and a Hollywood type. His rich, deep voice matched his appearance to perfection.

"Glad to meet you, Joey. And I'd like to tell you how much I enjoyed your performance. Jim Marshall is an old college buddy, and even though we don't see one another often, we do each other favors whenever an opportunity pops up. When he asked me to come down here tonight to look in on you, I really had a dozen other places to be. But I came, and I think he may have done *me* a favor. I'd rather not take your time now. I know you must be bushed. I'd like to give you this, and ask you to call me one day next week. Let's see if we can arrange an audition."

He handed Joey a business card which had a Bleecker Street address in the Village for The Living End—the best in new music and good food.

"Well, Jim, I've got to be going. Thanks for asking me down." They shook hands. "Good night, everybody. Nice meeting you. Oh, and Jim, if you ever find any others like this one, you get in touch, real fast. I'll pay for the phone call."

"You're good for a dime any day, Hal." Marshall smiled.

Golding left the stage and headed for the auditorium exit.

"Well, there, Joey Montagne, you guard that card with your life. It might mean something very special to you, very soon." Marshall put his arm around Joey's shoulder.

Joey realized that he had not introduced Mike and Papa or his mother to Mr. Marshall.

"Mr. Marshall, I'd like you to meet my mother, my uncle Mike, and my grandfather."

They shook hands.

Marshall addressed Mike. "Hello, Mr. Montagne. I've heard a lot about you. I'm glad you could come."

As Mike eyed Marshall, his voice erupted into a sneer. "So you're Marshall. I hear a lot about you, too. Joey's always sayin' 'Mr. Marshall this, Mr. Marshall that.' "

"Joey's a fine young man, Mr. Montagne. I'm glad to call myself one of his friends.

"I'm not sure a friend would be puttin' this actin' stuff in his head."

"I'm afraid the idea was there long before I came along. If I've done anything at all, I've tried to clear up Joey's notion that acting is an easy business."

"It's not *his* business, mister. Not the way I see it."

"That's not really my concern, Mr. Montagne. That's between Joey and yourself." Marshall stepped back. "Will you excuse me? I'd like to talk to some of the others." He said good night and walked toward the Martins who were leaving with their son, Tom, who had played the other father in the cast.

Lily broke the awkward silence. "Well, Joey, don't you think we'd better head for home? I've prepared some cold cuts, and there's some fresh cider Helen Woods brought back from upstate."

"We'll follow you in a little while," Birdie said. "You go on ahead"—hoping that by separating Joey and Mike, even for a few minutes, she might help to dispel the hostility that had dampened the evening's triumph.

Papa Montagne hesitated as the others started to leave. "Come here a minute, Joey." He grabbed Joey by the arm. In his hand was a five-dollar bill. "Take it, and don't give me a hard time. You buy Birdie one of those ice-cream sodas she likes so much. It's a special occasion. I only wish

Albert and your father could have been here tonight. They would have been as proud of you as I am. That's what I keep telling people, only they don't listen. We Montagnes are different. Each one of us. Yet we've got to be the best of them all."

"I'm listening, Papa. And thanks—for everything." Joey watched the old man walk toward his son and daughter-in-law.

"What was that all about?" asked Birdie.

"Oh, just some man talk. Come on, let's get this gop off me."

Back in the dressing room, as she helped Joey smear in the cold cream, Birdie couldn't repress her feelings.

"Boy, Mike is awfully hard to like sometimes. His whole world revolves around himself. Couldn't he try to be civil . . . just a little bit?"

"In a way, it's not his fault, Birdie. Mike is pure Mike. He just can't be a phony. He says exactly what he feels. You can't blame him for that."

"That's just the point," she answered. "Mike is *all* feeling. Like a thought would get lost in his head, or die of loneliness. He ought to try and think more often. It wouldn't hurt anybody—least of all, Mike."

"Wishful thinking," Joey said. "You know that old saying about wishing will make it so? Well, don't believe it. I've been wishing for years that Mike would understand me. Just *try* to understand me. We live in the same house, we're in the same family, but he's always far away, as though I've done something to him that he'll never forget. And the worst of it is, it's getting to a point where we can hardly talk to each other. He shuts me out. Ah, let's change

the subject. He's taken enough from me this evening."
Joey felt himself sliding into a depression.

"It's been *your* evening, Joey. He can't take that away
from you. And you know something? I do believe in wishes
coming true. I wished for your success tonight, and we
even get a bonus. Up pops that Mr. Golding from out of
nowhere. Who knows what can happen?"

"Things don't just happen, Birdie, you know that. Like
the show tonight. It didn't just happen. It's been a lot of
hard work. The kids who built the sets and managed them
backstage. Miss Hopkins' girls sewing like crazy, and the
kids in the orchestra playing like it was Carnegie Hall.
And Jim Marshall running around like a nut, seeing that it
all gets put together right. Sure, some of it must be luck,
but a lot of it is sweat and strain. I was just a small part of
it."

"Don't underestimate yourself, Joey. The kids all caught
fire from your performance. They leaned on you and it
worked beautifully. I know you brought a lot of pleasure
to a lot of people tonight."

"I wonder what Big Joe would have thought," he asked.

Birdie let the question go unanswered, not wanting to
break the moment Joey was sharing with his dead father.

"I haven't thanked you for all your help." He kissed her,
holding her strongly in his arms.

"Mmm. That cold cream smells groovy. And you know,
it doesn't taste too bad."

"Now! Leave the room, young lady, while I change. Be
with you in two minutes."

"Be my guest." They kissed again.

Joey changed and gathered his costume together, carefully hanging it in the wall closet.

They walked out of the darkened auditorium and into the night air. Intuitively, they knew they would want to visit the roof before they went downstairs to join the others in the Montagne apartment.

Even though the view from the roof was dimmed by a veil of clinging smog, the skyline and the bridges glowed softly, and Joey felt they had never looked more beautiful.

As the two peered out over the parapet, they could see the lights on the marquee of the Loew's Theatre, a few blocks away.

Joey decided to play the game he and Birdie had invented when he first knew he wanted to be a performer. They would take whatever names were on the marquee and substitute new ones in their place.

He began. "Jean Simmons and Joey Montagne in *The Robe*."

"Joseph Montagne and Elizabeth Taylor in *Raintree County*," she countered.

"Not bad! How about Joey Montagne and Henry Fonda in *War and Peace,* with Audrey Hepburn and a cast of thousands?"

"Pretty good! Try to beat this—Joey Montagne and Vivien Leigh in *Gone with the Wind* in Dixiecolor!"

They laughed.

"That's easy!" And Joey ended it as he always did. "Carol Channing and Joey Montagne, in *Macbeth, Baby,* a new musical by Cole Porter *and* Rodgers and Hammerstein."

They would always change the titles and the names, and sometimes they fell silent and didn't laugh—thinking that in some miraculous way it might someday happen.

As they trudged downstairs from the roof, Joey knew he might have a hard time keeping his temper cool in

Mike's presence. He just wouldn't let Mike have the satisfaction of spoiling what had been a memorable evening. And, as his excitement diminished slowly, he welcomed the thought of sleep—quiet, unthinking sleep.

5

THE PERFORMANCES OF *The Fantasticks* had gone beauti-
fully, and word had gotten around the neighborhood that
Joey's acting and his voice had found a perfect role in El
Gallo—that Big Joe's kid was really something on the stage.

Joey was gratified by the crowds of neighbors and
familiar faces he saw backstage after each of the four performances, tossing warm words of affection at him, like the
confetti that magically floated through the scenes of the
production. And at the last performance, that lovely moment of sadness made its way up from the audience and
across to the performers, and then back again, as each person in the auditorium knew that the last curtain had
closed, and that the light of reality had to replace the soft
pink and amber of the make-believe world the Plays and
Players had created.

On Thursday, almost a week after he had met Hal Golding, Joey was talking with him on the phone, making an
appointment to audition for The Living End. Golding suggested that Joey meet him at the coffeehouse late Friday

afternoon, after school. Birdie wanted desperately to go along, but felt that Joey ought to appear by himself, that somehow, it would be more professional that way. Anyway, she had agreed to meet two elderly Caughnawaga women, who were going to tape-record some material with her at the Neighborhood Center.

At about five o'clock, Joey went into the city on the subway, carrying his guitar and the good wishes of Lily and Papa Montagne. Mike knew nothing of the appointment, but not because anyone had hidden it from him. He had not talked much with Joey since last Friday, and they deliberately avoided a meeting.

Joey made his way up the stairs of the subway exit and into the city streets. Crowds of people, who worked in the tall, grimy loft buildings and factories, lunged and pushed their way, looking to Joey like automatons who had been set in motion by some mysterious hidden power. Unsmiling, bent by end-of-the-day fatigue, they were unaware of Joey and his mission. Yet, as he observed them, the vague shape of a song began to form in his mind, and he remembered a phrase he had read once in a biography of Jack London. Work beasts. Creatures locked into a daily trap, earning money for their needs but never to know the sense of dignity and accomplishment that could come from a different kind of work. He felt sorry for them and the millions like them, and knew that he could never choose that kind of existence for his own.

As he headed toward Bleecker Street and The Living End, his mood lifted. The bright lights of pizza places and craft shops and clothing stores, and a multitude of restaurants and boutiques with exotic merchandise from distant countries, gave the street the look of a constant carnival.

The only thing that spoiled it all was the river of refuse lining the curbstones, flowing out of the garbage cans piled against the walls of the buildings.

Standing like some small fortress in the center of the block between Sullivan and MacDougall Streets was The Living End. A huge sign, done in the rapid bulb-blinking manner of an old-fashioned movie palace marquee, spelled out its name, and a flamboyant black-and-white banner gently flapped in the breeze. LONNY ARLEN—THE ASTRONAUTS.

Joey had seen the young comedian on a recent television program and admired his use of a distinctly urban kind of humor which kidded the daily trials and tribulations of city residents. The Astronauts was a rock group, like many others, trying to find their own piece of fame, after the explosion caused by the Beatles.

Joey walked through the entrance of the building and paused for a moment at the small box office. A young woman, dressed in the current fashion, with granny glasses poised low on her nose, asked him, "Can I help you?"

"I have an appointement with Hal Golding."

"You and a hundred others," she remarked matter-of-factly. "Go right through there." She pointed to a huge blowup of Harry Belafonte, which practically concealed the door. He walked into a dimly lighted corridor and came upon two long Shaker benches on which a number of people were seated.

Joey noticed an empty space and sat next to a man dressed in a buckskin outfit, with a large, friendly face, and long hair. He moved over, making more room for Joey.

"Join the crowd, kid," he said jovially.

"Is this where you wait to see Hal Golding?" Joey asked.

"Yep. This is the place, and wait you will. That Golding feller must be mighty busy. I been here about an hour already. I ain't used to waiting so long for nobody back home."

"Where are you from?"

"Nashville. I guess you heard about it," the man grinned.

"I sure have. A lot of good music comes out of Nashville. Are you a singer?"

"Guess you could call me that. I'm right out'n the hills. Matter of fact, I cut some records down there, and this Golding feller heard 'em and wanted to see what I looked like. He flew down to Nashville and caught my act at a roadhouse. My agent down there thought this might be a good time to hit the big city, so I come up here for a week. You sure got yourselves one helluva town. I tell you that."

"You like it, do you?"

"Cain't tell yet. But it's sure got enough people and buildings. And guitars. Seems everybody up here makes music. I never in my life seen so many people carrying guitars. Why, look around you, right here. Seems practically everyone sittin' on these benches got himself a guitar. And some pretty fancy ones at that."

Joey leaned forward and looked down the corridor at the others sitting on his bench and the adjoining one, and everyone did seem to be coddling a guitar case. Some had even brought along their electronic gear to amplify the music they were going to make.

One group of young people caught his eye. Seated on the other side of the fellow from Nashville was a startlingly platinum-haired girl, dressed in the same costume as the three bearded men sitting near her. The men had long, dark hair, which each of them had swept severely back from their foreheads with a beaded headhand. They wore satin shirts, suede, fringed trousers, and beaded moccasins. Around their necks they each wore a large, colorful pendant in a sunburst design. The girl had added one distinctive feature to her appearance. From a thick braid of her hair, into which she had laced a red ribbon, hung a huge red feather.

The girl was aware of Joey staring at her.

"Hi," she winked at him. "We're the Seminoles."

—Seminoles? Not like any I've ever seen. Here we go again.

"Really? From Florida?" Joey heard an echo of annoyance in his voice.

"No, we're from Trenton. We just picked the name out of a book about Indians. The boys were always arguing about picking a name and I just adore Indians. I think they're cute." She was leaning forward, talking across the man from Nashville.

"Say," he told her, "you kids wanna gab with each other, why don't you let me switch places. Here, young feller, move over."

Before Joey could do anything to discourage the move, he found himself shifting closer to the girl, as the man from Nashville moved to the other side.

"You got a fire stick?" the girl asked Joey.

"A . . . what?"

"A match, honey. Aren't you onto Indian lingo?"

"I thought that was what Indians called a rifle."

"No, that's a thunder stick. Anyway, got a match?"

"Sorry, but I don't smoke."

"What's the matter, not old enough?" she said slyly.

"No. Smart enough," Joey responded.

"Oh, well, I guess it won't hurt me not to smoke before we go in for our audition." She opened the suede pouch that hung from her belt and dropped her pack of cigarettes into it.

"You got something against Indians? You sure look at us kind of funny."

"Maybe you're kind of funny to look at," Joey told her. "I bet you watch 'Wild Woolly West,' all the time."

Joey's first remark seemed to have passed her by.

"I just adore that program. How'd you know?"

"Just a guess." Joey was beginning to enjoy teasing her. "Have you ever seen a real Indian?"

"Only in the movies, or on TV. But they're among my favorite people. I just love the way they dress. It's so colorful. And I love their music, and the way they dance, and those darling tepees they live in. And their names—Crazy Horse, Sitting Bull, Bald Eagle. They're so romantic—not like my own, which by the way, is Cynthia Schultz." She paused to catch her breath.

—Cynthia Schultz, Seminole.

"And even if they were mean to our settlers," she continued, "scalping pioneers, and attacking wagon trains and all that, I still think they're cute."

Cute. Joey winced. He just had to slam that word back at her somehow.

"Do you think I'm cute?"

"What kind of question is that?" she said, eyes like a kewpie doll.

"You trying to be funny, or something?" one of her bearded partners barked at Joey.

"No, not funny. Just factual. The lady says Indians are cute, and I happen to be an Indian."

"What kind of Indian are you?" Cynthia Schultz asked.

"Caughnawaga."

"Never heard of it," she said blankly.

"Me either," said the beard.

"Is that my fault, or yours? I thought you were up on your Indians."

Joey felt the conversation had gone as far as he cared for it to go, and he was relieved when they were interrupted by a voice coming over a loudspeaker.

"Seminoles. Seminoles. Mr. Golding will see you now."

The group rose, gathered its equipment and began to make its way in gaudy procession to Golding's office.

"Good-bye," said the girl to Joey, "and good luck."

"Scalp them," Joey told her. "Give them a real scalping."

"You're cute anyway," she said as she disappeared through the door to Golding's office. "Maybe we'll meet again some time."

—Who needs it? Platinum-blonde Seminole with red feather . . . Princess Big Fake . . . Cynthia Schultz from Trenton.

Slowly, about every fifteen minutes, other performers were paged on the loudspeaker, and ushered into Hal Golding's presence. The benches were emptying fast, but not fast enough to suit Joey.

Then the loudspeaker voice announced . . . "Foster Calhoun. Hal Golding's ready for you now. Foster Calhoun."

The man from Nashville rose from the bench and turned in the direction of Golding's office.

"That's me, kid. Folks call me Foss Calhoun. You remember that name, now. I just might give the big city a taste of my kind of music. And who knows, these folks might just be smart enough to like it." He extended his hand. "By the way, I don't know your name. Guess you didn't offer it, or I didn't ask."

"Joey . . . Joey Montagne."

"Well, a heap of luck to you, Joey Montagne. See you around."

As Calhoun disappeared into Golding's office, Joey thought about all the people who had sat on the benches that day, waiting to display their ability for Hal Golding to judge. How many of them would make it, rewarded with a chance to perform for The Living End's audiences? For a few minutes, alone with his thoughts, he felt lonely and vulnerable, and wondered how many persons Golding saw each day, each month. What strange and unknown future lay ahead for the Seminoles, Foss Calhoun, and himself? Those unknown boys from the dock area of Liverpool had shook the world in their scramble from the slums to the stages of the largest cities in the world. They had started in the sleazy jazz clubs in Hamburg, where their music was slow to catch on, then back again to London, and the continent. But they were originals. And Joey knew that was part of the mystery. To come along at a time when there was no one to offer you competition. And if you were original enough, soon there would be a long line of imitators, never quite as good as the original, yet able to benefit from the impact the unique style had won.

He wondered if he had the quality that Golding was looking for and if he would be able to perform as well as he had the week before.

He would be the last to be called. He glanced at his watch and saw that it was nearly seven o'clock, and he was nervous and hungry, and anxious to get the audition over. And what about Golding's stamina? His ability to adjust to the different kinds of music he was hearing? Would he be just as tired as Joey was?

Joey Montagne.

Even the voice on the loudspeaker couldn't conceal its fatigue, that it, too, had come to the end of a long day.

He rose from the bench, walked down the corridor, and opened the door at the end.

Hal Golding was seated behind a large, handsome, modern desk, and the first thing Joey noticed was the wall behind the desk, covered from the edge of the ceiling to two-thirds down to the floor with glossy, framed photographs of two or three dozen personalities who had entertained at The Living End. Belafonte, The Kingston Trio, The Weavers, Dylan, Woody Allen . . . he was interrupted by Golding's voice and handshake.

"Glad you called, Joey."

"It's good to be here, Mr. Golding."

"Sorry it's taken so long to get to you. I never really know how long some of you people are going to take. Sometimes it's over in about five minutes . . . at least that funny little hammer in Golding's head tells him it's over. Kindness sometimes lets it go on a bit longer, until I tell them they're not what The Living End is looking for."

Joey heard an inner voice asking a question he couldn't ask out loud—What's it going to be for me?

Instead, he found himself asking Golding, "Can you tell me what The Living End is looking for?"

"Good question, Joey." Golding played with a letter opener. "I'd say the first thing we're looking for is a quality that sounds pretty corny, but it's very important to me and my audiences—sincerity. Anyone who gets out on that floor has to really mean what he delivers. Whether he sings or talks, he's got to reveal not only a talent that pleases, but a kind of honesty that goes along with it. I don't like any slick acts down here, and neither do the young people who come here for an hour or two of relaxation. I leave the smooth guys to television. That monster thrives on them, and gobbles them up faster than it can get them. We don't rely on any fancy tricks. We've got a simple but very effective lighting board, and the plainest stage you can imagine. In fact, I dignify it by calling it a stage. It's really just a platform. If you've got the stuff that will allow you to get out there and give them what they want, it works just fine. And they seem to know a phony, if and when I slip up. I think it's happened about twice in the last five years. But enough of this hot air. What would you like to do, Joey?"

"I thought I'd do 'Try to Remember' from last week's show." His voice was steady.

"Go right ahead." Golding leaned back in his chair.

Joey adjusted his guitar. He strummed the opening chords. His voice, soft and tremulous at first, soon found its register and the lyric made its way into the room, bouncing gently from the ceiling and the walls. It brought with it a warmth which the lyric writer and the composer had intended, and the song's feeling about a lost innocence and a world made beautiful by memory. Joey heard his final word and his fingers drifting to the closing notes.

"That was fine, Joey. Just fine."

To Joey, *fine* sounded old-fashioned, yet Golding was sincere, or at least his voice convinced Joey.

" 'I Gave My Love a Cherry,' " Joey said softly.

Again, the warmth came through. Golding seemed to be watching him more intently, and Joey ignored him, concentrating on the letter opener in his hand. Then, he remembered what Jim Marshall had taught him about establishing contact with one face, just one solitary face in the audience, and directing his entire effort to that face, as though it were the only one in the room. Golding was the only one in the room, so Joey lifted his eyes slowly from Golding's hand to his face. Joey's eyes met Golding's and the song seemed to lift itself effortlessly out of Joey's mouth, helped by his nimble fingering of the guitar. Everything seemed to be working, and the voice and the guitar conveyed the full meaning of the old folksong. After his last note, Joey heard himself sigh.

"All right, Joey. How about a change in tempo? Got something up?"

"Sure, Mr. Golding. How about 'Le Bateau'?"

"I don't think I know that one. French, is it?"

"Canadian. My grandfather taught it to me when I was a kid. It's about a race on the St. Lawrence to see which of the canoers gets to the trading post first. It's kind of fun to listen to, but not so easy to do."

And the words of a rollicking river song plucked their way from Joey's guitar and memory. When he reached the chorus, the lyrics tumbled out, tripping over themselves in comical, almost acrobatic fashion.

"I don't know if I got it all," said Golding, "something about a storm and a fire, and a large black bear, and a beautiful Indian girl. Am I right?"

"That's pretty good, Mr. Golding, for a first hearing."

"It was fun, Joey, and like a lot of tunes, I'm not sure you have to understand it to enjoy it. Why, I was singing

'Frere Jacques' long before I knew what the words were about. But tell me something, are you Canadian?"

"No, sir. I was born right here in Brooklyn. But we're Caughnawagas, who came down from Canada a couple of generations ago."

"That's Mohawk, isn't it? I should have guessed it. It's hard to pin down, but you've got a special kind of look. It's not that you look Indian. I think it's that you don't look like a lot of other nationalities or races . . . or whatever the heck we're calling them these days."

"Indian's okay, Mr. Golding. It gets kind of complicated. Caughnawagas are a branch of the Mohawk nation, which was part of the Iroquois Confederacy. Anyway, I'm a genuine, 100 per cent New Yorker."

"I like the idea of you being Indian. It's new and different. By the way, did you see the Seminoles out in the reception room? I didn't buy that stuff—100 per cent phony. Oh, they sang and played all right, but not much better or worse than a dozen other groups I've heard this week. That Indian get-up got me, though."

"Me, too," agreed Joey.

"That's what I meant before," Golding continued, "about wanting a basic honesty. You can't just impose an identity on yourself by dressing up in a costume. Looking like a gypsy certainly wouldn't fool anyone into accepting you as the real thing." He paused and then laughed. "Why, I had a group in here a couple of weeks ago dressed like monks. They called themselves The Levitation. And believe me, their act never got off the ground." He seemed pleased with his pun.

"Got another question, Joey. Do you have any original

material . . . you know, something you've written your-self?"

"Yes, I do, Mr. Golding. But I've never done them for anyone but my family or friends. I don't know if they're good enough for The Living End."

"Let me be the judge. What have you got?"

"Here's 'Fathers and Sons.' "

Joey sang the song, which was his own favorite, a simple but strong statement about the differences between generations.

"Pretty damn good," Golding reacted. "How about another?"

"I call this one 'Life Is A River.' " Again, a simple but effective combination of words and music brought Joey's idea into the open, and Golding's reaction was one of surprise and pleasure.

"You kids amaze me. You know, it used to be that young people were ashamed of writing poetry. They'd hide it in a drawer, and maybe never show it to anybody. Nowadays, I guess we're returning to the tradition of the old troubadours. You know, those medieval minstrels who used to wander through Europe singing their hearts out about the pain and pleasure they saw in the life people were living. If you don't mind, Joey, I'd like one more original, and then we'll call it day."

"This is my newest one, Mr. Golding. I'm not sure it's finished yet. I got the idea from a *Life* magazine article about a helicopter rescue team in Vietnam."

Joey's lyric told about young soldiers from different parts of the United States, whose lives were ended by the war. A farm boy from Pennsylvania, a miner from Minnesota, a black youngster from Louisiana. He called it "The Man You'll Never Be."

When he had finished he looked to Golding to bring the audition to a close.

Golding was pensive. He was obviously touched by what he had heard, and he sat there silent.

Joey opened the guitar case, and carefully placed the instrument inside. The click of the latch on the case seemed to bring Golding out of his reverie.

"They're very good, Joey. Not equally good, mind you. But you've got some good ideas, and you make the words and music match for the right effect. I've been in this business long enough to know an instinctive talent when I bump into it. You're pretty young yet, and you'll have to spend a hell of a lot of time polishing up. If you don't mind I'll show you what I mean."

He pressed a button on a console, partially hidden from Joey's sight, and Joey heard himself on tape, his thoughts, his words, his music.

"That has the makings of a very good song. It's a little bumpy here and there, but it smacks home where it should. You've got it building nicely toward the climax. Did you ever have training in composition?"

"No, Mr. Golding. I learned to play the guitar at school. I've always liked to write, and I guess it just seemed natural that I'd try to write some songs."

"It's not easy, Joey, but I think you're off to a pretty good start. If you'd like to stay and join me for a pastrami sandwich, I'd like to invite you to see the show. Our evening starts pretty soon, and I'd like to explain the details of your first contract. You've got yourself a two-week deal. Won't be for a couple of months, though."

Joey was startled by the good news.

"I'd love a pastrami sandwich, Mr. Golding. And I'd like to stay and see the show. But most of all, I'd like to call home. May I?"

Golding pushed the phone toward him. "Live it up, young man."

Joey wiped his hands on his trousers, so he could dial Lily without getting his fingers caught in the phone.

"Mom . . . Joey. No, everything's okay . . . and Mom . . . guess what?"

His mother's excited voice matched the smile on Golding's face.

6

When joey arrived home after seeing the show at The Living End, he overheard Mike talking loudly on the phone about an accident. Lily and Papa were also talking about it in the living room.

"Something awful happened to Buzz Gallagher at the Verrazano construction site," Lily said with deep concern, "Mike is talking with the hospital."

Joey wanted to hear more about Buzz's condition before he would tell them about what happened to him at the audition.

After Mike had finished on the phone, he joined the others in the living room.

"I told Buzz never to look up when he's standing under anything, but you kids just don't listen. You think you know it all. Well, that boy'll have something to remember the rest of his life. Accordin' to the doctor, he's darn lucky to be alive. They don't know what saved him."

"What happened?" Joey asked anxiously.

"He's been hit by a six-inch bolt that fell from a height

of about a hundred feet. It hit him in the face, and went four inches through his skin, just under his right eye."

"How terrible!" Lily was thinking about Anna Gallagher and how she must have taken the news of her son's accident.

Mike went on, "The bolt lifted his cheek, crushed his jawbone, and got stuck in his throat. I saw him out at the bridge before the ambulance took him away. What a mess!"

Joey felt the pastrami sandwich arguing its way up from his stomach.

"I'm going to meet some of the guys at The Longhouse," Mike said. "I got no heart for TV tonight, and I'm not ready for sleep. That damned kid! I don't know whether I feel more sorry for him or for his old man. Tim Gallagher must be worried sick." He left the room, slamming the door shut, headed for the bar that was the gathering place for the Caughnawaga community.

The talk about Buzz's accident had diminished the excitement about the audition, but Lily and Papa were anxious to hear the details before they went to sleep, so Joey told them his impressions of Golding, and about his enthusiastic reaction to his music and the exciting performances of Lonny Arlen, and the Astronauts.

Suddenly, he jumped to his feet and, with a graceful flourish, announced, "And now, ladies and gentlemen, the highlight of the evening!" He removed the contract from his jacket pocket.

Lily unfolded it nervously and waited for Papa to put on his glasses.

"You are sure you understand what you're signing?" Papa asked.

"Oh, I'm not old enough to be a legal contractee with my own signature. Mom will have to sign it for me as my legal guardian. Mr. Golding explained it all. It's pretty simple at this stage. He's offering me a two-week engagement to perform sometime in the future at The Living End, once every night, and twice on Saturday. I'm to get one hundred dollars a week."

"Joey . . . that's wonderful!" Lily's eyes mirrored her pride.

"And that's not all, folks. He would like an option on some possible recordings for some time in the future. And he also mentioned something about a summer stock theatre that he runs in Pennsylvania where I might try doing a lot of different parts during the season."

"Sounds like you've started, Joey, doing what you've been wanting to do. I'm happy for you, son," Papa told him.

"Joey, before I do any signing, maybe we could show the papers to the lawyer at the Ironworkers' Union, or maybe to Father Bello, or Mr. Marshall."

"Sure we could, Mom. That's a good idea." He sighed deeply. "And now, if you'll excuse your tired, old son, I'd like to just lie down and let the whole thing settle. My mind's buzzing a mile a minute."

"Good night, Joey. Get a good night's sleep. You sure earned it," Papa told him.

"Oh, by the way, Mom, did you get a chance to phone Birdie about the audition?"

"I did, Joey, right after you hung up. She was so excited, we found ourselves practically speechless. She expects to see you tomorrow morning."

Joey kissed Lily on the cheek, and then left them to go to his room.

The sharp arrows of the warm shower released some of his inner tension and he fell asleep enjoying a strange mixture of exhilaration and exhaustion.

7

THE NEXT MORNING, Birdie awakened early after having spent a restless night. Lily had phoned her shortly after having talked with Joey from The Living End, told her the exciting news about Golding's offer, and invited her to have breakfast. But Birdie had to refuse the invitation because she had set up a recording session at the Neighborhood Center with two of the oldest Mohawk women in the community who were going to tell her about the role of the woman in Mohawk society as they had witnessed it from the time they were children. Annemarie Rice was almost eighty-four and Clementine Foret was eighty, so the session sounded too valuable for Birdie to postpone. She asked Lily to tell Joey to join them at the Center if he could. She wanted to get an early start before the room got too crowded and noisy.

The Neighborhood Center, a large rectangular store on Atlantic Avenue, had once been a supermarket and an old-fashioned A & P grocery store. Although it had stood empty for a number of years, the neighborhood knew it was there, neglected and bare like some museum piece, never to be visited but, nevertheless, respected all the same.

When Father Bello, the young, progressive priest at St. Paul's, needed a place which would serve as a day-care center for children of working mothers and a tutoring center for school-age youngsters in the afternoons, the old store had attracted him because of its size and convenience. In a short time, he had convinced the neighborhood political organizations to pitch in and raise funds, with his help, so that the store could be utilized as the Neighborhood Center, at least for one year.

Jim Marshall had heard about the Center at a faculty meeting when Mr. Shapiro, the school principal, asked for volunteers who might help set up a tutoring program for secondary students.

One night at dinner Marshall mentioned it to his wife, Thora, who was a social worker with the New York City Department of Welfare. He thought her experience might prove valuable to the Center, and that she might be willing to offer her services gratis, since Father Bello's budget was fast being eaten up by the rental for the store, and government funds seemed to be tied up in red tape.

At school, he spoke to Bella Kowalski, who offered to tutor in math a few hours a week, and to Marvin Wall, who promised to do the same in science. He himself would handle reading improvement and general English.

Eager volunteers had come in to scrub down the store, to remove cobwebs and pieces of old plaster that threatened to fall. Old lighting fixtures were torn out and replaced by strips of neon tubing. The walls were whitewashed and hung with brightly colored travel posters donated by a local travel agency; visitors were uplifted by the happy glimpses of Paris, Rome, the Swiss Alps, and faraway Bangkok. Some of the mothers, who would benefit from the Center, sewed bright orange curtains for the two front windows, hanging them just high enough for privacy and low enough to let in the sunshine and natural light. At the rear of the store a small table held a hot plate for the warming of soup, food, or hot chocolate. On the floor there were cartons containing various games and puzzles. Furniture consisted of several folding chairs donated by a local catering service and some tables improvised by fitting long wooden boards over wooden horses. The place was clean and functional and, if the store did not retain any vestige of its former elegance as a grocery, at least it seemed alive again and anxious to be of service to all who entered.

For children still too young for school, it offered a haven managed by part-time women workers, who gave them care and attention. In recent months, it had served a new purpose, as a social center for senior citizens, where the older members of the community could come to sit and talk with each other, or read, or play cards or checkers, and get advice from Father Bello about any of their problems with social security or health.

When Birdie started her project, it seemed natural for her to use the Center as the place where she could meet with the Caughnawagas who were willing to cooperate in recording their folklore. She had just finished fixing the tape recorder, setting it up with a fresh reel, when the two elderly women arrived.

Annemarie Rice must have been a tall woman once, for even now, her posture seemed remarkable for a woman her age. She reminded Birdie of pictures she had seen of Eleanor Roosevelt, but with a light-brown, seamed face, and bright black eyes.

Clementine Foret was shorter, with a lovely head of still-black hair, only intermittently gray, which she wore in a thick coronet braid. Her face was like a wrinkled paper bag that had seen much use through the years but had proved too strong to be discarded.

"Good morning, Mrs. Rice, Mrs. Foret. I want to thank you for coming. Can I offer you a cup of coffee?"

"You mean that instant stuff?" said Mrs. Foret, pointing to the bottle near the hot plate. "Not for me, thank you. You young people want everything quick. You miss a lot by not doing things the old way, the slow way."

"Speak for yourself, Clemmie," Mrs. Rice told her companion. "I would like a cup. It's bad manners to refuse Birdie's offer, even if it isn't as good as your own coffee."

Birdie spooned coffee into the cup, added hot water, and stirred it, amused by the old woman's spunkiness.

"Sugar, Mrs. Rice?"

"No, Birdie, I like it as strong as you can make it."

She handed Mrs. Rice the dark, steaming cup.

"Now, ladies, I'll explain what I'm trying to do. I'm collecting all kinds of material about life on the Caughnawaga reservation, especially as you knew it when you were young. I'd like very much to hear about family life, and the way people spent the holidays, Mohawk or Christian, and recipes, and about the songs and dances, and the stories that were passed on to you from the generations before you. I don't think anybody has ever done this quite the way I'm attempting to do it, and all you have to do is ignore the microphone and machine on the table.

Just talk with me as though we were sitting in your kitchen. Do you have any questions?"

"Not me," said Mrs. Foret.

"Or me," said Mrs. Rice, sipping the cup of coffee.

"Tell me when to start, Birdie," said Mrs. Foret.

Birdie pressed the switch and signaled the old woman. "Go right ahead, Mrs. Foret."

"Well, I'm getting too old to keep secrets any more. Birdie, your mother's been after my recipe for corn soup for a long time. I guess I've been selfish, not wanting to share it with anybody . . . not that your own grandmother doesn't make a good one herself."

"Mrs. Foret, do you remember how it used to be made up in Caughnawaga? Grandma tells me it's changed quite a bit down here."

"Yes, I do remember, Birdie," she smiled. "The main difference is down here we use pork, while up there, when I was a girl, my mother used a bear's head."

"A bear's head?"

"That's what I said, Birdie. And it sure gave it a delicious flavor that our corn soup just doesn't have any more."

"Could you tell us how you make it?"

"Sure. Now let's see. You bring about three quarts of water to boil in a large kettle. When the water is boiling, you add the corn and some wood ashes—you know, the kind you gather from a fireplace. Let the mixture boil a while and keep stirring it until the hulls come off the kernels. You got that, so far, Birdie?"

"Yes, Mrs. Foret, you're doing fine," Birdie smiled.

"Well, then, you'll see the kernels swell up. After the mixture has boiled a bit, rinse it with a colander three or four times. That should remove all the wood ashes and hulls. Then put on fresh water to boil, add the corn and some kidney beans, and a pig's head. Allow the soup to simmer until the pork is cooked real well, and the whole thing is good and thick. And there's your corn soup . . . better than any in the whole world."

"Aren't you the modest one, Clemmie!" Mrs. Rice told her. "Mine's made slightly different, and I bet it's just as good."

"You're too old for me to argue with, Annemarie, so I'll just take your word. Come to think of it, you've never invited me to taste your soup."

"I haven't made it in years. Arthritis cuts down your puttering around in the kitchen, or your daughter-in-law does. I just don't cook any more, but that doesn't mean I don't remember," the old woman told her friend.

"That was wonderful, Mrs. Foret. And you really tasted it when they used a bear's head instead of pork?" Birdie asked.

"I did, Birdie. And it was a beautiful soup. Seems to me, we've gotten so far away from the old ways, we've lost a great deal."

"Now, Clemmie, where in the world are you going to go up to the meat counter of Bohack's and ask for a bear's head?" Mrs. Rice laughed.

Birdie clicked the stop button on the recorder.

"Mrs. Rice, I've heard that some of the members of your family were once members of the False Face Society. Am I right, and could you tell us about it?"

"Yes, that is correct, Birdie. Oh, it goes back a long way, back to my great-grandfather. I don't know if I remember everything, but if you let me shut my eyes, I somehow see it all better."

The old woman placed one hand across her eyes, as though by blocking out the present, the past would become more clear.

Birdie started the machine.

"We've been Catholic way back since those early missionaries. It seems strange that the old ways of the medicine societies were still popular when my great-grandfather was alive. You know what our people believed in those days, about illness? They thought that sickness could come from a breakdown in a person's health, like a sore throat, or catching a cold. But they also thought that illness came from offending the supernatural spirits, which upset the balance of harmony with the world. When a person fell ill, the family would call on a member of a medicine society to help bring about a cure, since those members had been ill themselves at one time, and had been cured.

"My great-grandfather was one such member, and in our home we still have the mask he wore. It's a comical looking thing, which I think would have made me laugh, but the older Caughnawagas respected its power, and I guess I shouldn't mock it. I heard tell how the mask, and the man who wore it, were offered tobacco and mush, in return for the curing ceremony.

"I remember one of those ceremonies. It was performed for a young boy who had fallen through some thin ice while fishing one winter. I guess he had what folks call pneumonia nowadays—he was feverish and flushed, and could only lie there coughing and having a hard time trying to breathe.

"My grandfather, who was also a member of the False Face Society—I guess he, too, had been cured of a serious disease—was called into the small cabin where the boy lay in bed. The old man started chanting in a strange language I'd never heard before. It was high and nasal, and soon he began to circle the boy's bed, singing a song that sent shivers through my spine. The mask was on his face, and it glowed in the light from the fireplace because he had rubbed it with sunflower oil to assure its power. They burned tobacco in the fireplace and then the old man rubbed the hot ashes from the fire between his hands and then on the head of the boy. The singing continued for a long time, and I was ushered away, as though to have outsiders there could spoil the work of the False Face.

"Two days later, the boy's fever had broken, and in a week, he was up, running around and ready to play lacrosse.

"I don't know to this day how or why the False Face worked its cure, but I think it has a lot to do with the respect the patient had for the mask and my grandfather. I guess the whole thing was scary enough to work, like what we call faith healing nowadays."

The old woman paused. "Is that what you wanted to hear, Birdie?"

"That was wonderful, Mrs. Rice. I want to thank you both."

The door of the Center opened, and Joey stood on the threshold. He walked to where Birdie sat with the women.

"Hello, Mrs. Rice, Mrs. Foret. How are you?"

"Mrs. Foret can tell you how we are, Joey. I'm just about catching my breath," Mrs. Rice told him.

"We're as fine as two old ladies can be," Mrs. Foret said jauntily.

"Don't go calling me an old lady, Clementine. Speak for yourself. Ever since Father Bello told us we were senior citizens, that's what I want to be called."

"Well, pardon me," said Mrs. Foret. "I wouldn't want to hurt the feelings of my oldest friend."

"Every time I open my mouth, seems I put your foot in it," Mrs. Foret smiled.

"Birdie, I'm sorry to interrupt what you're doing," Joey apologized, "but I just dropped in to say a quick hello. Billy's asked me to go out to the new Verrazano tower. Mike has invited him to go up on the elevator, and he feels it's a great opportunity to take some photographs. He needs help with his equipment, and I'd like to help him out."

"Take care, Joey. You know how upset you get when you go up high."

"Yeah, I know. One of these days I'm going to have to visit a shrink or somebody to help me get it out of my system. I know that the vertigo's going to happen, and I'm a big enough boy now to have gotten over it. But it still happens. I'll be miserable, but your brother is my best friend, and I really want to do him the favor of going up in the tower. If I look a little green when I get back, have pity and offer me a lot of affection."

"You'd get that even if you didn't look green. Take care," she repeated.

As Joey left the Center, Birdie thought of the irony . . . that one of the Montagnes should have a paralyzing fear of heights. She wondered if the old False Face Society members might have helped him with a cure.

"Ladies, are you willing to go on with the recording?"

"Might as well," said Annemarie Rice. "If I go home, I'll only be in my daughter-in-law's way. It's nice sitting here and talking with you, Birdie."

"It sure is," agreed Clementine Foret, "and if you won't get angry with me, Birdie, I'd like a cup of coffee."

"That's you, Clemmie Foret, always changing your mind."

"That's a privilege of the old . . . excuse me, senior citizens," the old woman answered her friend.

8

ANXIOUS TO GET to the Verrazano construction site, Mike hurried through breakfast and headed for the nearest candy store for a copy of *The Daily News*. On the second page he found the story about the accident. It was accompanied by a photograph taken at the hospital, after Buzz's face had been treated. The usual pretty nurse was at his bedside, looking admiringly at the young apprentice ironworker, whose grateful eyes were the only visible part of his head, buried in bandages.

Mike grew impatient waiting for Billy and Joey to arrive, and he mauled the newspaper, unable even to concentrate on the sports pages. Suddenly, the boys were standing alongside the car.

"Finally! I thought maybe you forgot," he barked at Billy.

"Sorry we're late, Mike," Billy apologized.

"Well, let's not waste any more time. Put your stuff on the back seat." He held up the centerfold section of the newspaper. "Here it is. What do you think of it?"

"Be with you in a minute, Mike," said Billy, carefully placing the large black box with his equipment on the back seat.

Across half of the centerfold was a large, magnificent photograph of the newly completed Brooklyn tower of the Verrazano-Narrows Bridge, the one they were going to visit.

"It's beautiful," Joey remarked, "really beautiful."

"Wowee!" exclaimed Billy. "And to think I've been working on that!"

"So was Buzz Gallagher," Mike snapped. "I hope you know better than that, Billy. You ever let me catch you actin' smart-alecky and takin' chances, and you're gonna find yourself flat on your can. If your father can't beat some sense into you, maybe I can." The boys were silent.

He gunned the motor and they were off, speeding through the streets of Gowanus, heading for the Belt Parkway.

"Gee, Joey, the guys are still talking about the show and how much they enjoyed it." Billy broke the silence.

Joey recognized the sincerity in Billy's compliment, knowing that many of their neighbors and the ironworkers who had attended the performances had never before seen a Broadway musical.

"How're you doing on the job, Billy?" Joey asked, changing the subject.

"He's doin' a good job," Mike interrupted. "If he keeps it up, he might make one of the teams. Maybe next year."

"It's great, Joey! You know how you feel when you're up there on the stage? Well, that's how I feel up on the bridge. It makes you feel like a midget . . . the thing is so darn big! We must look like ants at a picnic . . . runnin' all over those beams. I've been up a number of times, carrying coffee and water. You can't believe how the world looks from way up there, Joey." Billy's voice rose in wonderment.

"I can believe it, Billy—believe me, I can."

They were passing the Brooklyn waterfront, already busy with its morning hubbub, huge transport vans swallowing up the loads of cargo from freighters anchored at the docks.

The sun was touching the city with fingers of pale pink and orange, pushing the gloomy gray clouds across the far horizon. The Manhattan skyline was a giant stained-glass window, tossing thousands of rainbow reflections into the morning air. Traffic on the parkway was light and they arrived at the bridge site twenty minutes later.

Mike parked the car. He waited for the boys to unload the back seat. Billy strung his used Nikon 35 camera around his neck. In his hand, he held an 8 mm. Bell and Howell motion-picture camera. Joey carried a smaller box with lenses, the tripod, and extra film. The three of them walked down a dirt road to the anchorage.

To Joey, the massive equipment, the rows of steel beams, the work shacks looked strangely deserted. Yet he knew that in a few hours the construction site would resemble a hospital waiting room, with dozens of the ironworkers milling about, like the proud relatives of the new-born infant, taking pictures, shaking hands, congratulating each other on their soaring triumph over the elements. The completion of the Brooklyn tower was a monumental accomplishment.

"You ready, boys?" Mike asked. The two were lagging behind.

"As ready as I'll ever be," thought Joey, following the

other two as they passed the watchman's shack, waved a quick hello, and walked toward the waiting elevator at the base of the tower.

As the elevator door slammed shut, Joey felt the old familiar sensation start in his toes and make its way up to his knees. The car zoomed up to the top of the tower, eighty stories up from the ground.

Up, up. Steel. Space. The air hissed by them, and Joey heard it whisper . . . Big Joe . . . Big Joe.

When the door opened, Joey was overcome by the vastness of the tower's interior. Its skeleton was made up of thousands of steel boxes, stacked in a complex pattern. It was a miracle of design and engineering.

The Verrazano-Narrows was going to be the world's largest span, each tower tossing into space tons of steel, millions of rivets, and as many bolts, all strung together to link Brooklyn and Staten Island in a symbolic marriage.

As he looked at the walls of the tower shimmering in the sun, Joey thought how much it resembled diagrams in his biology book. The men even called each of the units a cell. Like some gigantic protozoan, the huge derrick, mounted on rails bolted to the tower face, made its way upward, planting thousands of cells to the surface.

The wind was gentle. Joey inhaled gratefully. The three looked out over the harbor and the city, each wanting to store up the magnificent view against some day in the distant future when they could share it with someone who had not been there with them.

The bay looked like a huge, fat, green-brownish blanket —smooth, except for the white creases left behind by three tankers ploughing their way through the channel. Uptown, a cruise ship, chalk-white, luxuriously allowed two tiny tugs to push it slowly away from the land, into mid-river.

Joey thought about the view from the top of the Empire State Building, which he had visited on a field trip with a class when he was younger. Even then, he had not dared to walk to the edge of the building, though there was a railing. He had viewed the city through one of the telescopes anchored to the floor and found it an awesome sight.

Here, on the tower, he felt as though they were floating in space, unhampered by any construction anywhere near it. He hoped Mike had not seen his clenched fists, or the cold sweat which covered his body and made him shiver beneath his thin windbreaker.

"Well, Joey, whadda' y' say?" Mike asked, patronizingly.

"It's magnificent, Mike. Really, you almost can't talk about it."

"That's just what I was going to say, Joey," Billy said, "only you beat me to it."

"Drink it all in, fellas. I don't know how often we can come up here again." Mike swept his outstretched arm, encompassing the sunlit horizon as though it were all his.

"Thank God," Joey whispered to himself, feeling with each step as though his legs were weighted down with a ton of steel.

"You kids better get goin' with your pictures. We ain't gonna be up here all day, you know," Mike bellowed.

Immediately Billy, with Joey's help, set up the tripod. Soon he was busy clicking away, first in one direction and then another, adjusting the Nikon, fastening on the lenses, taking readings on a light meter. To Joey, it all looked very professional, and he respected the seriousness with which Billy tackled the marvelous views of the city and the harbor.

"If I can only nail some of these views down on film, I'm sure going to enter them in as many contests as I can. There aren't too many guys that will ever get this opportunity," he told Joey.

When he was finished with the still camera, he worked with the Bell and Howell, surveying the views like some mad astronomer sweeping the heavens to discover new stars and planets.

"I guess that does it," he announced, his voice filled with satisfaction. "And I want to thank you, Mike, for letting me come up here."

Mike silently puffed on a cigar, not even acknowledging Billy's gratitude. He seemed far away, on some distant cloud of thought, and Joey wondered whether Big Joe was somewhere in Mike's mind.

The boys gathered Billy's equipment together. In a few minutes, they were on solid ground again.

Walking toward the car, they were greeted by Tim Gallagher, Buzz's father, the head of the Union's apprenticeship program.

"Hi, Tim," Mike said. "I'm sorry I didn't get to see you in all the excitement yesterday. I couldn't make it to the hospital. How's Buzz?"

"Saints be preserved, he'll be all right they tell me. It's a miracle, that it is."

"I'm glad," Mike said, slapping Tim on the shoulder. "He's a darn nice kid—even if he is careless."

Tim agreed, telling them, "When I first saw him at the hospital, I didn't know whether to slam him one or kiss him."

"Sure was lucky," Mike told him.

"Sometimes I wonder if we do the right thing by our boys, Mike. Making them do what we do. 'Cause it's good and easy for us doesn't mean it'll be that way for them. Maybe Joey's got the right idea, tryin' for the Union's Cole scholarship. It'll see him through college, or give him a good head start."

Tim's words hit Mike like a hot rivet.

Joey looked straight into Mike's face, knowing the moment had come unexpectedly. But he was relieved as he felt the burden of the secret leave his chest.

"What scholarship?" Mike asked Tim.

"Lily was in the office a few weeks ago, pickin' up an application for Joey. I think he stands a good chance— bein' that he's a fine student." Tim didn't know that he was the first to tell Mike about it.

"Funny how you never know what's going on in your own family—under the same roof!" Mike said angrily.

Billy jumped in for his friend. "Joey told me about it, Mike." Unknowingly, he had added fuel to the fire.

"Isn't that nice! And since when are you responsible for Joey?"

"It's not that, Mike. Joey's different. We all know it. He just isn't cut out for ironwork. He's good in school—lots of us aren't. I love bein' a boomer, and besides, I never wanted to go to college. Joey's different, Mike. Can't you see that?"

Billy as amazed at his own courage in speaking up to Mike.

"You keep your trap shut about what Joey's good for! Mind your own business, you hear, Billy?"

Tim came to Billy's defense. "The boy don't mean no harm, Mike. And I'm sorry if I started somethin'. I know you been wanting to get Joey into the apprentice program, but when I saw Lily, I thought you'd changed your mind."

"Everybody changes my mind for me," Mike snapped. "First Lily, then Billy . . . who the hell are you all?" He rushed past them, toward his car.

Tim Gallagher, surprised by Mike's reaction, turned to the boys. "Talk about the temper of the Irish. Your Uncle Mike has us beat. But he'll get over it, Joey. I've seen him stewin' before. It takes a little while for his boilin' blood to cool down. He's lucky he don't blow himself up. Well, I got a hundred things to do, boys, and only a few hours to do 'em in, so I'll be sayin' so long." He turned and walked off toward a group of men gathered at one of the equipment shacks.

As the boys approached the car, Mike started the motor, revving it loudly, reflecting his anger. The boys walked fast, knowing that it would be just like Mike to drive off spitefully, leaving them behind.

As they hurried, Billy turned to Joey sadly. "Gee, Joey, what're you gonna do?"

"I wish I knew, Billy . . . I only wish I knew."

They sat in stony silence as Mike drove. They didn't know where he was headed, but in a few minutes they pulled up outside The Longhouse, the Caughnawagas' bar. Nancy Larue, wife of the owner, was mopping the floor as they entered. Mike skirted the area puddled in suds and headed for the bar.

"So early, Mike?" Nancy joked, as he passed.

"So what?" he replied, gruffly. He ordered a double bourbon. Nancy leaned her mop against the wall and walked behind the counter.

"I can't serve the boys. They're underage."

"Give 'em sodas."

Joey and Billy ordered Seven-Ups.

Mike turned to Billy. "Say, Billy, do me a favor, will ya? Move over there, to one of those tables. I wanna talk to Joey."

"Sure, Mike." Billy picked up a copy of *Playboy* lying on the counter and walked away.

Mike took Joey's arm and gruffly led him to a table. They sat, staring, while Mike began to drum on his glass.

Joey dredged up enough courage to break the silence. "Uncle Mike, I was going to—" He stopped. *Uncle* sounded phony.

"Don't give me that 'uncle' stuff! I wonder what Big Joe woulda said if he knew you were stabbin' us both in the back—both of us!"

"That's not true, Mike. If you'll only calm down and listen to me for a few minutes, I'll try to explain."

"Snakes don't explain nothin'."

"Mike, do you want to talk, or don't you?"

"I've got nothin' to say. You wanna talk—go ahead."

Joey found himself lost for a few seconds. How do you begin? He took a deep breath. "I'm chicken, Mike. I could never be an ironworker. Like Big Joe. Like you."

Mike was unprepared for his nephew's open frankness.

"Whadda ya mean? There's never been a Montagne who's ever been chicken! Not your grandpa, not your father. You're talkin' outa your head." He looked at the floor.

"No, Mike. I'm trying to make sense, for the first time."

He told Mike about his acrophobia and how it had come to him since his father's sudden death. He looked straight into Mike's eyes as he spoke, hoping to find even the dimmest glow of understanding. But Mike's eyes were empty and as he listened to Joey's confession, his jaw grew taut, making his face a stone barrier. He had placed his hands over his ears, almost as though to drown out the sound as the boy continued, pleading, explaining, trying to breach the stone wall. Mike fidgeted, making wet circles on the table top with his glass and then suddenly wiping them out with a quick swipe of his arm. Finally, Joey came to a halt.

The disgust was evident in Mike's voice as he spoke to Joey.

"Maybe me and you haven't got much to say to each other, Joey. I know I'm ashamed to hear what you just told me. And I'm glad Big Joe's not around to hear ya. We've always been strong. Nothin' could lick us." He rose, a tower of pride, walked to the bar, and ordered another drink.

When he returned, Joey said, "I'm sorry, Mike. I know that doesn't mean anything to you. But try and understand. I'm not like you, or Papa. I'm not like Big Joe. You're in ironwork because you like it, or need it. I just want the chance to be myself and do what I want with my life. Maybe I won't make what *I'm* trying for, but nobody should take the chance away from me."

"You mean actin', don't you? Painted-up fags! I hope

you fall flat on your ass. It'll serve you right. Then you'll come back, squealin' like a sissy, askin' me for help. And it'll be too late."

"Mike, have you ever thought what you would have done, if you didn't like ironwork, or if you couldn't have done it?"

No one had ever asked Mike that question, and it hit him hard, clanging in his mind like a rivet falling into a pail.

"Whadda ya mean, didn't like it? Or couldn't do it? Whadda ya take me for, some little yellow punk, like you? From the first day Papa took me out with him on a job, I was glad to be with him, and with your father, too. We always were the best. When Papa got old and hadda stop, it was Big Joe and me. I've been waitin' a long time for you, and I've been waitin' for nothing. You make me puke. You don't deserve to call yourself a Montagne. Someday, if you want me to look ya in the face, it'll have to be up in the air, on some unfinished job, when you get the guts to be a Montagne again."

He rose quickly, pushing the table away from him, and walked to the door. He glanced at the sign over the lintel: THE GREATEST IRON WORKERS IN THE WORLD PASS THRU THESE DOORS.

As Mike opened the door, Nancy Larue was shouting in the phone booth.

"Oh, my God! When did it happen?"

Billy rushed toward the booth, followed by Joey and Mike.

She hung up the receiver, dazed, on the edge of tears. In a rapid staccato, she repeated the news she had just heard. ". . . an accident! Last night. On the way to Canada.

Henry Riviere is dead! His kid, Johnny, and Fred Lachaise
are hurt bad, real bad!"

Every time an accident occurred, whether it happened
on a construction job, or on the road going to and from
the Caughnawaga reservation up in Canada, the impact
rippled through the community. The brave little colony,
having made a life for itself in Brooklyn, seemed to grow
smaller each year, and every fatal accident was another
message of its mortality. To the older Caughnawagas, it
appeared that their former, gentle life had given way to a
destiny compounded by speed and height; their sons and
the families of their sons would never know the ancient
beauty of the chase, or the sweet victory of the hunt.

Joey wondered what Mike and Billy were thinking,
when the three again sat in the car, completely deflated by
the tragic news. He didn't know how they would handle
the knowledge of the accident. He only knew how he felt,
how he wished they would get home quickly so that he
could go to his room and lie down. There, in the dark, he
might find some silent answer to the mystery of why so
many of his people seemed haunted by a desire to be the
best, to excel, to be the strongest, the fastest—even if it
caused their deaths.

Joey found it hard to accept the reality that Henry
Riviere was only a name now, that the tall, husky man
whose joy in being alive, whose raucous laugh delighted
all who knew him, had met his doom in a shower of
splintered steel and hot oil. And he thought of the widow
and her children, and how empty their days would be
without a husband and father. A wave of memory swept
through his mind and he heard the echo of questions he
had asked . . . "Where is Daddy? Why won't we ever see

him again? Mommy, why are they putting Daddy in the ground?"

Joey knew that some of the questions would eventually be answered. And the answers understood. But never the ultimate question—why?

9

As WITH THE OTHER tragedies—accidents on the hazardous drive to Canada, or those which happened on construction sites—the news of Henry Riviere's sudden death swept through the neighborhood like brushfire. In a few hours many Caughnawagas, friends and neighbors of the dead man, visited The Longhouse, where a collection was taken up for the expenses of the immediate family. Accident or death always brought out an almost forgotten feeling of tribal communion. On the mirror over the bar were hung several notes of gratitude from widows and orphans of those who had passed away.

Sunday, at St. Paul's, attendance at all three masses was high, as it always was after a tragedy. Father Bello announced from the pulpit that the Riviere funeral service and burial would be held at the reservation on Tuesday. The Ironworkers' Union had chosen Mike to act as its representative, and he would be driving up to attend the services.

As Birdie and Joey walked into the street, leaving the

gothic gloom of the church behind them, the neighborhood seemed as gray as their mood.

"I feel sorry for the kids," Joey said. "It's bad enough
for Marie Riviere, but it's so unfair to the kids."

Birdie's face mirrored her anger. "Why do they keep
up that insane idea that they're just as good behind the
wheel as they are with their rivet guns? You'd think grown
men would know better."

"Let's face it, Birdie. They drink too much for their own
good. Maybe some of them are more alcoholic than they
care to admit. And that drive can get as boring as hell,
especially after dark with mile after mile of nothing but
concrete staring you in the face. They get too eager to
get it over with, so they nip at the bottle and speed ahead
at ninety an hour. You do that often enough, and you're
bound to get too relaxed. That's when it happens."

"I wish there was some way someone could get to them,
to show them how foolish their ways are. And maybe to
help them change."

"That's a big order, Birdie. But maybe we could talk to
Father Bello about it. Possibly he could help."

"You know, I keep thinking what a wonderful place the
Neighborhood Center is, since it started. Maybe they could
run a clinic . . . or maybe Alcoholics Anonymous could
start meetings, or something."

Joey knew there was no easy answer to be found, and
that so much of the way the Brooklyn Caughnawagas lived
had become a deeply ingrained habit. From the time he
had been a child, he knew that many of them had been
killed during their frantic automobile trips between Brooklyn and the reservation, which stood on the southern shore
of the St. Lawrence River, just above the Lachine Rapids,

about nine miles upriver from Montreal. The big, heavy, expensive cars they drove were no guarantee of safety, and almost as many Caughnawagas had died in roadway accidents as had been killed on construction jobs all over the United States.

Like homing pigeons, some mysterious, inexplicable force guided the Caughnawagas back to the reservation, for visits to their families and friends, and it seemed as they grew older, or moved farther away from Canada, the visits became more important and more frequent in number.

Joey thought about Henry Riviere's funeral, and felt a deep desire to attend, as though by being in the dead man's presence, his last day on earth, he might find some illumination for his own life.

As though Birdie were reading his mind she turned to him and said softly, "I'd like to go up to the reservation, to Henry's funeral. I haven't been there for a long time, longer than I really remember. I'd like to see how it's changed, and if it wasn't an intrusion, I'd just like to wander around with my tape recorder, describing it all."

"You belong there just as much as anybody else. I guess that means going up with Mike. We'd better ask him real soon. We don't have too much time."

After their last talk, Joey wondered if Mike would be receptive to anything he asked for . . . but he couldn't refuse their request.

They walked slowly, silently, not knowing how to talk themselves out of the depression which had grown steadily since the church service.

As they approached the Center, they saw the Marshalls'

station wagon out front. Joey opened the store door and walked in, Birdie following.

"Hi, Mr. Marshall, Mrs. Marshall."

"Well, good afternoon, Miss Le Brun, Mr. Montagne," said Marshall with a broad smile of welcome.

"Working on Sunday?" Joey asked.

"Yes, how come?" Birdie added.

"It's not really work," Marshall answered.

"Can't think of any place we'd rather be on a sunny Sunday afternoon," Thora Marshall chirped brightly.

"Well," said Marshall, pointing to a large carton nearby, "don't just stand there, you strong, healthy things! Give an ailing man a helping hand."

"Ailing is right. He'll probaby be up all night with an aching back, and if there's anything I enjoy it's staying up all night rubbing him with liniment and listening to him moan and groan."

"Hush, Mrs. Marshall. That *is* your name, isn't it? At least, that's what's on the marriage contract, and it says in sickness and in health."

"Honey, you should have married a nurse, not a social worker. I think 'The Fantasticks' started him with an ulcer, now he's breaking his back, and watching the tutoring program going down the drain is making him really nervous. And when he gets nervous, I get nervous."

"Mrs. Marshall, why do you want to burden these children with our problems?" he told her with mock seriousness.

"Can we really help?" Joey asked.

"You sure can. Bend into that carton and tell us what you behold," Marshall answered.

Joey lifted a large heavy volume. "I behold encyclo-pedias. Britannica, no less."

"Encyclopedias," Birdie echoed. "Where'd they come from?"

"One of our neighbors was ready to toss them into the incinerator. Luckily, we got there just in time. We sure can use them around here. I bet some of our clients have never seen the inside of one of these things."

"And how many times have you added joy to your life by reading an encyclopedia?" Mrs. Marshall asked her husband.

"You don't go to these things for joy. You need reference books for problems you encounter in your studies, but it's the whole business of training them to do research that I'm after. You know yourself, that somewhere along the line you've got to stand on your own two feet and learn where to look, and how to look, and what to look for. These things can come in mighty handy, for historical information, for biography, for a hundred and one things."

"Don't get on the defensive, Mr. Teacher. I thought you were having a hard time getting your kids to come around here, nevertheless jumping into encyclopedias."

"Which reminds me, Joey, when we're finished with things," Marshall said, "can we just sit and talk for a few minutes about the tutoring program and why you think it might not be working?"

"Sure, Mr. Marshall, I'd be glad to, if you think I might be able to tell you anything."

"Well, I've got a strange idea that asking a student about other students and their behavior might be a step in the right direction. You know how it is with education . . . I mean with a capital E. You get a hundred experts giving you a hundred very scholarly opinions, but no one thinks of asking the kids themselves."

"My, my, how serious we're getting, for a Sunday afternoon. I was just thinking that we ought to put up a plaque somewhere, in honor of that incinerator." Mrs. Marshall proposed.

They laughed, knowing that ever since the Center had opened, many of the Marshalls' neighbors had unwittingly contributed to its furnishing with discarded items headed for destruction in the fiery bowels of their apartment buildings. Two lamps, a magazine rack, a bookcase, two years of old *Life* and *National Geographic* magazines, and a giant fern plant, left like an abandoned half-dead infant, but now flourishing in the front window.

While Birdie wiped the books with a damp cloth, Joey and Mr. Marshall arranged them in order on the bookshelf.

Thora Marshall called to them from the hot plate on the table in the rear of the store, "Coffee, anybody? Come on, now, you can't let a girl drink all alone. Tell you what, after we have our little board meeting, how about a general retreat to a nearby ice cream parlor for a soda or sundae?"

Joey liked Mrs. Marshall. If she sounded sharp or sarcastic at times, he reminded himself that as a social worker she probably saw people at their worst, saw things that could sour a person's viewpoint about life and luck.

When they had finished their work, the four of them sat down at one of the long tables which rested on wooden horses.

Marshall began. "Joey, why do they call the Center the dummy store?"

Joey hesitated. Dummy store. The phrase rode around in his mind.

"I guess it's just the idea that it's a special place where kids can go to get help. They hate to be seen going in or out of the Center. Maybe it's a matter of pride, because if you come here, you're not doing well at school, and it's no secret. I've heard kids refer to the Center as the dummy store, and they said it snottily, as thought it's an admission of weakness on their part to get help from anybody," Joey told his teacher.

"You know what that reminds me of, Jim?" Thora Marshall addressed her husband. "The food stores we used to have back in the thirties, when a lot of people were on relief. People used to go to those stores for food staples the government made available to them, for the stamps they'd turn in. But many of our neighbors had a real stubborn streak of pride, although they were just as hungry as the others. They'd sell their food stamps rather than be caught going into one of the stores. It was too public for them. I guess the average person doesn't like to be seen going to a public place for help. Perhaps it's too close to an admission of defeat. It's just too filled with personal shame for many of them to cope with."

"I remember it only too well," Marshall answered. "My family was on relief and were tickled pink that there was some place we could go for help. I guess it depends on the individual."

"Well, we've got a problem. We can't keep the Center so private or secret that the kids feel protected. They sure work hard at putting it down fast enough. We might as well call it the Gowanus Leper Colony. Dummy store!

Maybe we're the dummies for expecting them to come here at all," Thora responded.

"Joey, Birdie, we need your help," Marshall appealed. "We've got to get to work changing the image of the Center or, at least, making the kids feel that failing in school isn't a sign of some deep, incurable disease. School's the most important thing in these kids' lives at the moment. It takes up most of their time, and some of them just can't take the announcement on a report card that tells them and their families that they're failures—that they haven't got what it takes to accomplish the goals we've set for them."

"There's a lot of truth in what you say," Birdie offered. "Some of your goals aren't realistic—not for a lot of kids. Maybe the goals have to be changed. Maybe school's got to change."

"In some of my classes, I get the message loud and clear. The kids think society is sick. All they hear about outside is war and poverty and racial conflict. Some of their compositions and some of the class discussions make it sound as if life isn't worth anything any more, so why go on with an education that prepares you to join a sick society?"

Thora Marshall agreed. "They're not too far wrong, Jim. I guess they're still too young to realize that they've got to change themselves before they can hope to change society."

Marshall got up and peered through the front window. "Why don't they show up? Don't they know it's for their own good—that we're here trying to help, Thora? They can't move an inch toward a decent life without at least a high school diploma—even the packers down at the supermarket, and those kids shoving carts around in the garment center might not get those jobs without a diploma."

"Oh, they know it, honey," Thora answered. "But you know what's happened since World War II—*money*. They think it's the magic key to everything they'll ever need or want in life. Cars and clothes. Flash-in-the-pan. It's sad, but I'm afraid it's true. They can't see that schooling—some kind of education—can get them a one-way ticket away from a meaningless existence. So few of them have any plan for the future. They just want to live it up *today*, here and now."

Marshall unleashed his deep frustration. "Sometimes I think I understand why they feel that way. But, tell me, Thora, didn't we have problems, too, when we were kids? Every generation has its own beasts to conquer. Why don't they realize we're trying to give them the best weapon a kid can have—self-respect, the strength that comes from within, not the stuff he buys with a charge account!"

"Whoa there, Jim-Boy, simmer down," Thora warned.

"Guess you're right, honey. No use sounding off, if they're not around to hear it. We don't need the message, and they do."

Joey had been listening to the Marshalls, impressed with their sincere desire to help the neighborhood's school failures and dropouts. He had never heard his teacher talk about the Center with such a deep sense of defeat, and wanted to help if he could. But how?

"How's it been going this week, Mr. Marshall? Any better than last?" he asked.

"Not much. Only seven—all week. I'm going to have a hard time influencing my colleagues that it's worthwhile coming around here. They've got better things to do with their time than just sitting around waiting for the kids to show up. You know, Joey, Mr. Shapiro gave me a list of thirty-six names . . . all of them dangerously close to flunking for the year. Why don't they get off their backsides and do something to help themselves? Don't they care?"

Birdie found her chance to say what she had been thinking. "I don't think failing means anything to them, Mr. Marshall. It's like they've cut themselves off from everybody, from everything that means success to their parents . . ." she hesitated, ". . . to your generation. They think they're keeping their cool. As though it were a sin to admit that you're weak in something."

"Well, I don't know how strong we can be either, in the face of failure. Let's face it, kids. The tutoring program is being flushed right down the drain."

"You are absolutely right, my dear husband, and we had better do something about it real fast. I've told you what I think you have to do." Thora sounded impatient.

Joey's curiosity took over. "What's *that,* Mrs. Marshall? Excuse me, I didn't mean to butt in, but what do you mean?"

"Oh, it's all right, Joey. I can repeat it a hundred times more, if I have to. I've told him repeatedly, if I've told him once—he's got to reach someone in the neighborhood, a person the kids look up to, a hero, in their eyes. If a person like that tells them to get over here for their own good, they'll listen."

Jim Marshall answered with emphasis, having heard her plea many times before. "I've heard you, honey. And I've thought about it. But darned if I know *who* that magnificent cat is—where he lives and breathes."

Birdie and Joey looked at each other, both sharing the same instantaneous thought.

Mike Montagne.

Could they approach him to help with the Center?

Would he?

He seemed to fit the description Marshall had given them. Yet his antagonism toward Marshall, his constant battles with Joey . . . could he step outside himself to help them save so many of the neighborhood kids who were in trouble?

"That cat, Mr. Marshall, may be living at my house," Joey said excitedly.

"You don't mean—?" Marshall already knew the answer to his own question. He looked at Thora, and then at Joey and Birdie, and the four of them shared the knowledge that very soon one of them would have to get up enough courage to approach Mike and ask him to give the Center another chance to do the job for which it was organized.

"Sir James Marshall," Thora said, trying to hide her own doubts, "since you are, without doubt, the oldest and bravest amongst us, we charge you with the slaying of this particular dragon."

Jim smiled at his wife's remark.

"Lady Thora, how can you send this tired, old knight into battle with just a smile?"

Thora kissed him on the cheek.

"If it will help you at all, kind sir, rest assured that I am right behind you."

"That's what I figured," Marshall joked, ". . . way behind."

10

As JOEY PASSED the building where the Rivieres lived, he saw a large wreath of lilies tied with purple and black ribbons hanging from the front door. A house visited by death, he thought, with the lives of those inside changed, suddenly, permanently.

When he reached home the house on Schermerhorn Street seemed empty and strangely quiet. Papa and Lily were sitting in the kitchen and Joey noticed that the table was set for three. He wondered if Mike had come home after church.

"Are we ready to eat?" Lily asked. "I'm afraid I've settled for ham sandwiches and a salad," she apologized.

"Are you all right, Mom?" Joey asked.

"Your mother's been upset since she heard the news about Henry. I told her not to bother fixing anything fancy, Joey," Papa said.

"I'm not too hungry anyway, Mom. I probably killed my appetite with an ice cream soda Mr. Marshall just treated me to."

"Where'd you see Mr. Marshall?" Lily asked.

"Down at the Center. Birdie and I were walking home from church, when we saw their station wagon out front. We helped them unpack some stuff they brought over, and then we got to talking about the tutoring program. I hope I haven't kept you waiting. Where's Mike?"

"He's gone down to The Longhouse. He's pretty shook up by what's happened. One thing right after another," Papa said. "First, Buzz Gallagher, and now, Henry."

Lily put a platter of sandwiches on the table, then a large bowl of salad. She poured hot tea into their cups.

"Help yourselves." Her voice sounded sad and tired.

They ate silently, and finished quickly, as though eating were an interruption of more important things.

"Mom, do you think Mike would take Birdie and me along to Caughnawaga when he goes on Tuesday?"

Lily was surprised by Joey's question. "I didn't know you wanted to go along, Joey. And Birdie, too?"

"We've been thinking about it since church this morning. I've got a funny feeling that I ought to go up there. I don't know why. Birdie would like to visit the reservation for her report . . . you know, sort of describe what it looks like."

"Joey, I say you both can go along. Mike doesn't know it yet, but I'm going too," Papa said. "I don't know how many more trips I'm going to make before my final one. I'd like to see some of my friends, and our cousins. And I've really been yearning for a breath of that good Canadian air. I'll just tell Mike he's taking us along. That's all there is to it."

Joey was relieved to hear his grandfather resolve the problem of approaching Mike and asking for the ride.

After the dishes had been cleared, Joey grabbed a towel and offered to help Lily dry them. She stood at the sink, her hands buried in the soapy water. She handed him the rinsed dishes.

"Joey, the application is on your dresser. When you've finished go check it to see that I've signed in the right place."

"I will, Mom. Thanks."

"I hope I'm doing the right thing for you. First, signing the contract for Mr. Golding. Now, the application for the Union scholarship. They're big things, Joey. I hope . . ." She seemed to gag on the words which were caught in her throat.

"It's the right thing, Mom. You'll see." Joey hoped his confidence would help his mother through her uncertainty.

"Well, anyway, it's a beginning, Joey. You've got a right to that."

It's a beginning. His mother's words sounded stronger and he thought of the strange directions in which people's lives were fated to go. It's a beginning. He thought about Henry Riviere and the tragic waste of life . . . the ending.

Monday had been like any other Monday at school. Mr. Marshall had asked Joey when he thought Mike might be available for their talk about the Center, and Joey told him about the trip to Caughnawaga. Mr. Marshall decided to wait until later in the week.

At home, Joey got lost in the pages of a Faulkner novel that he was finishing for an English report. He was glad to interrupt the tortuous prose when Lily called him down to dinner. Despite Lily's attempts to draw Mike and Joey into conversation, tension hovered over the dinner table.

After the meal, Joey went back to his room, kicked off his loafers and tackled the Faulkner again, when he was distracted by the sudden blare of a television commercial. He closed the book in disgust and thought about going to the Center to finish his reading, but then realized that he had better talk with Mike about the trip before they started, or it would be a painful experience for all of them, Birdie and Papa as well.

He opened the parlor doors quietly and walked to where Mike sat.

"Mike, can I talk to you for a minute?"

Stony silence.

"It's about the funeral at the reservation."

Mike leaned forward, switched channels furiously, but still said nothing.

Joey tried to glue himself to the floor to prevent himself from kicking either the TV or the chair in which his uncle sat. He closed his eyes, cleared his throat, and tried again. "I'd like to explain why I want to go along. Can I?"

Mike glared at him. "Why?"

"I'm grateful that you're taking us along, and I thought maybe you'd like to know why I want to go."

"Look, kid, if you're so chicken you've got to have the old man tell me to take you and Birdie along, I don't need to know nothin' else. Funny, you got a big mouth when it comes to school plays. I don't give a damn why you wanna' go along. You just be ready at four in the morning, and don't keep me waitin', ya hear?"

Joey's blood boiled up into his head and he knew he was standing there with clenched fists. He didn't notice his mother in the doorway.

"Mike," she said, "he wants to go because he hasn't been

there for a long time. He'd like to visit Big Joe's grave."
She was not sure Mike would be convinced, but she knew
it was no lie. Joey would visit the cemetery.

"That's just great!" Mike's voice was bitter. "What's he
expect? Big Joe's gonna slap him on his back, and tell him
how great he is for wantin' to desert the Montagnes, for
wantin' to become one of them Hollywood fags?"

Lily was hurt by the crude way in which Mike took her
explanation and poisoned it with his own anger.

"Mike you're not doing your brother's memory the honor
he deserves, always jumping on his son this way. I know
you have your differences, and all I ask is that you stop
trying to be his father. His father is dead." She turned and
left the room, sobbing. Joey followed her.

Mike shouted after them. "What the hell am I supposed
to say? I'm sorry? Then, OK, I'm sorry!" He slammed the
doors closed.

Joey followed Lily to her room.

"That fink! That lousy fink!"

Lily was dabbing at her eyes. "Enough, Joey. I've had
enough."

"Are you all right, Mom?"

"I'm all right," she said quietly. "He can upset somebody
better than anyone else I know. I guess I'll never get used
to it."

"He shouldn't talk to you that way."

"That's Mike. I guess he'll never change. Joey, don't you
think you ought to go to bed? You've got to get up real
early. I hope we didn't disturb Papa."

"No, Mom. He's all right. I saw the light on in his room.
He must be reading his newspaper."

"Why don't you tell him good night, and then get to bed yourself?"

"Okay, okay." Joey knew his temper still made his voice sound irritable and edgy and he didn't want to leave his mother that way.

"Good night, Mom. See you in the morning."

"Good night, Joey. Sleep well." Lily kissed him on the cheek.

On the way to his room, he stopped at his grandfather's door and tapped softly.

"Come in. Why, it's you Joey," the old man said, looking up from his newspaper.

"Just wanted to say good night, Papa."

"I don't know if I'm going to get much sleep tonight, son. I didn't think I could get this excited about going up to Caughnawaga, and though it isn't a happy occasion, it'll be good seeing some of my old cronies."

"Well, don't stay up too late. It's a long drive and we're starting about four. You don't want to get yourself all tired out between no sleep and nearly ten hours in the car."

"I just hope Mike doesn't drive like those other maniacs. Seems to me we've got plenty of time to get there for the funeral at four in the afternoon."

"I'm sure he'll be careful, Papa."

"Never can tell with Mike," the old man said. "But here I am, keeping you from getting to bed. Go on now, and get a good night's sleep."

Joey felt his head hit the pillow, and it seemed to him that his whole body hissed, like a large teapot letting off steam. He picked up the Faulkner from the table where he had left it. In a few minutes, his eyes were weighed down by the long convoluted sentences and he fell asleep.

An old-fashioned alarm clock jolted Joey into wakefulness at three o'clock. He had thought to use the clock-radio which woke him each morning for school with news and music, but he knew this particular middle-of-the-night awakening could not be gentle and easy.

It clanged until he found the tiny lever to silence it. He showered and dressed in a warm, comfortable suit and took his raincoat with him for warmth against the cool, early morning air.

Papa was waiting downstairs, sipping the last of his breakfast coffee. On the table was a full meal which Lily insisted Joey eat. Orange juice, warm rolls, scrambled eggs and bacon, cinnamon buns and coffee.

"Feel's funny, eating so soon again," Joey told his mother, who sat at the table, dressed in the warm bathrobe he had given her the Christmas before.

"Never you mind. You'll be grateful you ate well when you're on the road. Mike's gone to pick up Birdie. Listen, Joey, this is for the trip. I just put together some things I know you all like. It's better than those places along the way." She pointed to a large shopping bag resting against the wall.

Joey glanced at the kitchen clock. 3:45.

"Well, I guess I'm as ready as I'll ever be." He rose from the table. "Take care, Mom. We'll see you soon."

Lily stifled a yawn. "You take care, Joey . . . Papa. Please."

"Now don't you worry, Lily," Papa assured her.

A few minutes later, as she watched from the front window, the Chrysler disappeared down the street.

The streets were dark and empty of traffic. Mike drove fast. They zoomed past huge trailer trucks which, at that hour, were more numerous than cars on the road. The Parkway . . . the bridges . . . the harbor . . . the tall buildings lighted for the many night employees busy cleaning them and making them orderly for the day workers . . . the dark night giving way to the pale hour before dawn.

Soon the vertical patterns of the city changed into the horizontal suburbs, and the smoky haze to the cloudless sky that hung over rolling hills and valleys. The Thruway . . . an endless ribbon of concrete pushing through rock formations, as though laid down by some giant hand. The car sped along, and its occupants were silent, as though talking would be a violation of the peace and beauty of the nocturnal landscape.

The steady purr of the engine was hypnotic, and Joey closed his eyes, slipping into a light sleep he seemed powerless to fight.

Suddenly, with the click of a button, Mike unleashed some loud music. It woke Joey with a start, but it also drowned out the monotony of the purring engine.

"Do you have to play that thing so loud, Mike?" Papa asked.

"Nope. Don't have to play it at all," Mike replied. He turned off the radio. Silence.

"Have you seen Buzz at the hospital, Mike? How's he doing?" Birdie asked.

"He's doin' okay. They'll be lettin' him go in a few days." Silence.

"The car sure rides beautifully, Mike," Joey told him.

"Glad you like it," he answered with an edge of sarcasm.

Mike seemed to stifle all attempts at conversation, and so they rode in silence.

About three hours after they had started from Gowanus, Mike pulled over at one of the service areas to give Papa a chance to stretch. Joey and the old man walked to the men's room. Birdie took the opportunity to peek into the shopping bag Lily had given them.

"Would you like a cup of coffee, Mike? Lily's sent along the thermos," she asked.

"That's a good idea. Her coffee beats theirs by a mile."

Birdie opened the thermos and poured Mike some coffee. When Joey and Papa returned, she poured cups for them and herself.

"Can't get over it. Look at that stuff come out steaming hot. The guy who invented that sure gets my thanks," Papa said, grateful for the good cup of coffee.

Birdie took the cups when they had finished and walked to the ladies' room to rinse them out. When she returned, Joey suggested they switch seats in the back. The Chrysler sped off, joining the stream of traffic which now seemed to thicken as the sun rose.

Birdie told Joey of her plan to walk through as much of the reservation as she could, talking into the mike in the style made popular by so many television reporters. She hoped she might even interview some of the residents, asking them questions which might add pertinent information to her report. Joey listened attentively, offering to help her in any way that he could.

They watched the road signs swiftly fly by. To Papa, the Thruway was a miracle, and he seemed to nod his head often, making a funny clicking noise with his mouth.

"This sure is some road. Must've cost them a pretty penny . . . but it sure is worth it, every cent of it."

They were surprised when Mike announced that they would stop for lunch, eating it in one of the service area parking lots. Joey's stomach had been grumbling for quite a while, and he was glad to dig into one of his mother's generous sandwiches. The second one tasted even better, and a luscious apple topped off the simple but delicious lunch. The others ate theirs with the same enthusiasm, Papa choosing a banana for his dessert.

"Those apples look good, but there comes a time in a man's life when his dentures tell him he's better off with something soft."

Mike pulled the car into the gas station and had the attendant fill the tank and check the front and rear tires.

"That's one thing that's changed. These guys don't do nothin' unless you ask them to. And it's not 'cause they're too busy," he complained.

As he had predicted, they approached St. Martine at about two o'clock. Twenty minutes later, they were at the Caughnawaga reservation.

Papa and Mike headed toward the small frame house occupied by Chief Twelvetrees, a Montagne cousin who lived on the main highway.

Joey carried Birdie's tape recorder, walking close to her side, while she managed the small microphone.

"I guess I'd better just jump in . . . huh, Joey?"

"You're on, Birdie. Go ahead."

She lifted the microphone to her mouth and tested the volume.

"Testing . . . testing. How is it, Joey?"

"Fine."

"The reservation is really not much to see," she began. "All in all, I guess it to be about four miles of farmland, swamp, and scrub timber. The main highway running from Malone, New York, to Montreal is the main street of the village. Nobody would pay much attention to Caughnawaga, or even know that it is a reservation. There are several small frame houses, and grocery stores and filling stations. But travelers and tourists are attracted by the ramshackle booths in front of some of the homes where you can buy Indian souvenirs like beadwork belts and bags, papoose dolls, moccasins, baskets, and gaudy pin cushions.

"The mailboxes in the front yards have names like Bigriver, Threeax, and Brownleaf, which are the English versions of the original Indian names." She paused for breath. "These names are sometimes left in their French version which the missionaries gave the original residents many generations ago, like my name Le Brun, which means the brown one, or Montagne, which means mountain."

She pressed the stop button. They were approaching the Twelvetrees' house.

The Chief, with his brown and wrinkled smile, was obviously pleased to see Papa and the younger visitors. He invited them in for some refreshment, which they refused, explaining that they were not hungry. Mike asked if they might head toward the church.

A few minutes later, the Chief and his wife had joined the Montagnes and Birdie for the drive to St. Francis Xavier, the largest building in the village.

They parked near the church, and when they got out, Birdie and Joey walked slowly behind the others. She clicked on the machine and described the church.

"St. Francis Xavier's was built by Jesuit missionaries about one hundred years ago. It is a popular stopping-off place for tourists. Pilgrims have attributed miracles to the relics of Kateri Tekakwitha, an Indian martyr who died at Caughnawaga at a very young age in the year 1680. She is still called the 'Lily of the Mohawks.' "

The church was filled with Caughnawagas, and a place had been reserved for Mike and the visitors from Brooklyn in a pew behind Marie Riviere and her children.

The solemn tones of the funeral Mass started soon after they were seated. Marie Riviere began to weep, a pitiful figure in black dress and veil. Many of the women in the church were looking at the Rivieres, reminded of other times when many of them had worn the clothes of mourning.

The funereal notes of the service echoed softly through the spaces of the church, and Joey was surprised when he heard the priest conducting the service in the Mohawk tongue rather than traditional Latin. He was unaware that the privilege had been granted many years ago.

As the singsong mingling of the voice and language wove itself into Joey's consciousness, somewhere in the corner of his mind the small door of an almost forgotten memory opened.

As Joey looked around the church, faces and forms near him became blurred. Looking toward the altar, he could see the pew where Marie Riviere sat with her children, staring at the coffin covered with a simple Indian blanket. He felt a slight dizziness and tried to concentrate on the blanket. The church was warm and incense filled the air with its musky heaviness. He glanced at Marie again and was not surprised that what he now saw was the image of

Lily Montagne as she had looked that day, sitting in the same pew at Big Joe's funeral. She was holding the small hand of the boy sitting next to her. Joey saw that small boy was himself, clutching his mother's hand to shield him from the unknown terror there, in front of him. Once more, he was attending Big Joe's funeral and, again, the casket loomed upward toward the high, vaulted ceiling of the church, dwarfing the child who understood little of what was happening at that moment.

The small boy watched the coffin in front of the altar. As the service for Big Joe ended, six Caughnawagas walked down the center aisle toward the coffin. Lily was standing, sobbing, and Mike supported her with one arm around her. As the men lifted the coffin to their shoulders, Joey broke away from his mother and ran toward them.

"Daddy, don't go! . . . Daddy, where are they taking you?" He was kicking and pulling at a pallbearer's legs.

Mike rushed from Lily's side and grabbed the small boy, lifting him, screaming and kicking, into the air.

Mike put a big hand across the child's face, lifting his head until their faces were pressed closely together. He growled into the boy's ear. "Keep your mouth shut! Don't cry, Joey . . . you hear! You're a big boy. You're a *man*. And Montagne men don't cry! Ya hear?"

The small boy was terrified by his uncle's strength, and as the whispered words drove their way through his stifled sobs he knew only one thing: this man, his Uncle Mike, was letting those men take his father away. Mike turned, gripping the boy's hand, and started walking up the aisle toward the exit. Just in front of them, Joey could see women surrounding his mother, who was blindly stumbling along behind the coffin as it was carried from the church.

Later that day, in the early evening, when his mother was tucking him into bed at the Chief's house, she spoke to him. He recalled how exhausted and pale she looked, her eyes grief-stricken.

"Good night, Joey. Your Daddy told me to tell you to be a good boy, and he asked me to kiss you good night." She was barely able to finish speaking, when she heard the young voice from the pillow stammer.

"Teh—teh—tell Daa—Daa—Daddy good night for me, too, Mommy. Wh—whuh—when will Daa—Daa—Daddy come home?"

The years drifted past Joey on a cloud of incense and now he was watching six other men lift Henry Riviere's coffin to their shoulders.

As the crowd left the church, Joey remembered that the procession would walk through the village, bearing the coffin, until it reached the burial ground atop the hill at the southern end of the village.

Ever since 1719, when the settlement became the permanent home of the Caughnawagas, Indians had been buried there when they died, even though they might live as far away as San Francisco or Miami.

As the procession moved along, Joey walked near Papa and Mike, who seemed lost in their own thoughts. As they passed the small frame houses with their television antennas and shoddy souvenir stands, Joey felt ashamed of the village and of what had happened to the once proud Caughnawagas. "They look phony," he thought. "A tourist attraction. Beggars who've forgotten their nobility." He saw a sign which made him wince with disgust.

STOP! POW WOW WITH ME
CHIEF TWELVETREES—MOHAWK SOUVENIRS

His own cousin, his family—a silly looking old man, selling souvenirs.

"Why does it happen?" Joey asked himself, knowing the answer was not a simple one, nor an easy one to find. The reasons spun in his mind, coming to a clear, concise halt.

The white man, believing his way of life to be the best, the only one, the right one, had brought it to the Indian. And with it came sickness, disease, the robbery of their lands, the whiskey ruination of their best warriors, and the sapping of their strength and dignity. What now remained of the Caughnawagas squatted beside the roadway, living up to the white man's image of his Indian brother. A foolish, phony-looking, feathered businessman selling fake Indian souvenirs.

Joey was glad some of the Montagnes had escaped to the high steel where, at least, a man could show his skill and strength. Big Joe Montagne . . . Papa Montagne . . . Henry Riviere . . . the dying sons of a vanishing race.

And yet, as he watched the procession climbing the hill, in his heart he was content that he would not join the ironworkers, that he was going to find a new way to spend the precious years and months and days of his life.

At the cemetery, Joey could see that the burial would be just like his father's, even though Henry had not died on a construction job. For the Caughnawagas who died in high steel, a simple gravestone could not tell the story of their daring and triumph. Instead, their graves were marked with lengths of steel girders made into crosses, and the few steel crosses erected in the beginning had now grown into a small forest.

After the coffin had been lowered gently into the ground and Joey was able to hear the earth covering it, he turned away and walked to his father's cross-marked grave.

Birdie and Papa had noticed his departure, knowing where Joey was headed. They stayed with the procession as it walked back to the cemetery entrance.

Joey looked down at his father's cross and then slowly knelt to pull at a few weeds that were pushing their way through the mound of earth.

He knelt there, communing with his father, knowing his father would hear.

"Big Joe . . . Dad . . . help me. Dear God, how I need your help." It was a silent prayer.

Joey waited. A few moments later, as he arose and turned to join the others, he knew what it was he would have to do—to show Mike that he was still a Montagne, that Big Joe's son had the courage of his convictions.

11

A<small>T THE CHIEF'S HOUSE</small>, after the service, the Montagnes
and Birdie were invited to share a simple supper with the
elderly couple, and then to spend the night. Papa was
grateful for the invitation, and looked forward to wander-
ing through the village with the Chief and dropping in on
some of his old friends.

In the center of the dining room stood a time-worn,
wooden table which the Chief had built many years ago.
They were all seated around it when the Chief's wife
brought a large bowl out of the kitchen, filled with a
simple but delicious stew which she poured over a generous portion of Indian bread on each of their plates. Birdie
and Joey asked for second helpings when they had finished.

"It's the best stew I've had in a long time," Birdie told
the old woman.

"Thank you, Birdie, but you should be no stranger to
this stew. Your grandmother taught me how to make it,
many centuries ago, when we were girls. How is your

grandmother? Does she have the same aches and pains all of us old women have?"

"Yes, I'm afraid she does," Birdie told her, not wanting to mention her grandmother's constant wish to come back to Caughnawaga to die among the people she had left so many years before. She looked at the old Chief and his wife and was impressed by the serenity in their faces, as though they had been spared the tension and worry her grandmother found in New York.

"What is that machine I saw Joey carrying, Birdie?" the Chief asked.

"It's a recorder," she answered. "I'll show you how it works when we've finished."

"I'm afraid we are finished," he apologized. "Maybe it is a blessing that old people do not have large appetites, for our cupboard is not always full, and my old lady sometimes is not feeling good enough to cook as she did when she was younger, even as young as a year ago."

"Shame on you," the old woman told her husband, "first for complaining, and more so for talking about us as though we are starving. We are glad to share whatever we have with family or friends. Thank the Lord there are always enough tourists to buy what we sell, although they do seem to be less each year."

She cleared the dishes from the table with Birdie's help, and placed a large tray of fresh peaches and apples on the table for dessert. For Mike and Papa, the Chief brought out an old crystal bottle of blackberry brandy.

"I think you'll like this. I made it myself. It's mighty good when there's a chill in the air." His eyes twinkled with mischief.

"Have you noticed how many days and nights are chilly

when you get to our age?" Papa asked him, pouring himself a healthy glassful.

"À *votre santé*." The old man lifted his glass.

"*Le même à votre*." Papa returned the toast.

They downed their drinks with a relish that pleased Joey and Birdie, who had not heard Papa speak French for a very long time.

Mike rose to his feet, after quickly drinking two glasses of the brandy, and excused himself, telling them he was going down the road to one of the filling stations, which also served as a billiard parlor, to talk with some of his friends.

Papa felt the effect of the brandy sooner and more strongly than he expected.

"I think I would like to lie down for a little while, Pierre," he told the Chief, "but only if you promise to awaken me in half an hour. I want to walk with you to see many of our friends."

"We would have invited them here to visit with you, but there is not enough room for all who would want to come. Go rest, old friend, I will wake you in half an hour. I want to see this machine the young ones have brought with them."

He walked Papa to his own room, and led him to his own bed.

"But, Pierre, have you enough room for all of us, to spend the night?" Papa was concerned.

"Yes, yes. It may mean a little moving around, and Birdie and Joey and Mike might miss the comfort of their own beds, but tell me, how many years has it been since you have slept more than four hours a night?" It was more a shared confidence than a question.

"You are right, Pierre. I see that what happens to us old ones in New York happens to you here in Caughnawaga, too."

"Go rest. We will talk later, and in the early hours of the morning while the younger ones still sleep." The Chief closed the door of his room gently.

Birdie was delighted for the opportunity to show the Chief and his wife how the tape recorder worked, and she and Joey asked the old couple numerous questions about how they lived and how their lives had changed through the years. Their answers were filled with a charm and humor that seemed to lessen the depressing reality of their existence.

The Chief glanced at the old clock on the mantelpiece.

"Listen. There it is. The half-hour chime. Sometimes I do not know whether man invented time, or time invented man. I do know we never have enough of it. It is time to wake your grandfather, Joey. Shall I do it, or will you?"

"Sit there, Chief. I'll do it." Joey walked to the bedroom and knocked on the door.

"I hear you. I'm up. A little cold water on my face, and I'll be out there in a minute," the old man called.

Papa and the Chief left the house to make their rounds of the village. The Chief's wife was busy in the kitchen preparing some of the special corn soup, *o-nen-sto*, which she wanted to send back to Lily. Birdie sat at the table where she and Joey talked into the recorder, describing what they had seen of the village, the funeral service, and the cemetery.

The evening ticked itself away on the mantelpiece clock which had just chimed eleven-thirty when the old men returned. By midnight, the house was dark, and the occupants were all asleep, except for Mike who was still out somewhere in the village and for whom they left the front door unlocked.

The ride back to Brooklyn was uneventful, and each of the passengers seemed content to sit wrapped in quiet thought about the funeral, the visit with Chief Twelve-trees, the walk through the village. Birdie was elated to have been able to record her impressions, and the inter-view. Joey's thoughts were a mingling of past and future, and he felt a deep sense of relief in having visited Big Joe's grave. Papa Montagne had loved the precious hours he had spent with his relatives and friends and wondered when they would see each other again. One thought, par-ticularly, pushed itself forward in his mind. What kind of life would he have had if he had stayed in Caughnawaga and not become an ironworker? Was he right to have made of his sons what he did? Even Mike was aware that his father and Joey and Birdie wanted the quiet, so he did not play the radio. He occasionally lighted a cigar, keeping his foot on the accelerator, determined to reach Gowanus as soon as he could.

The landscape sped by and soon the familiar sight of the George Washington Bridge loomed on the horizon, stretching like a concrete ribbon across the Hudson River.

They joined the smooth line of traffic heading across the bridge. Papa, admiring the span, said, "I forget what a good job this one is, and that a lot of our boys back in Brooklyn worked on it, too."

Mike paid the toll and then complained, "Ya know one of these days the Union oughta' get smart enough to get us some kinda' pass, so we can ride across the things we build without havin' to pay a toll. We put plenty of hours of sweat into the damn things. It don't seem fair. I wonder if the engineers and the guy that designs these things hafta pay every time they go across."

The suburbs soon flattened into upper Manhattan and the serpentine twists and turns of the West Side Highway. Three large ocean liners were docked at the midtown piers, and Joey strained to read their names as the car drove by . . . the *France,* the *Queen Elizabeth,* and the *Rotterdam.* Their huge bulks looked deserted now, but Joey thought of the hundreds of passengers who would soon be boarding them for voyages to magic cities across the Atlantic.

They were swallowed into the Brooklyn-Battery Tunnel, and emerged into the final stretch of the long drive from Caughnawaga to North Gowanus.

Mike dropped Birdie off first, and Joey helped her with the recorder, telling her good-bye at the foot of the stairs leading to the front door.

Lily was relieved to see them, and while Joey and Papa made their way to their rooms, she detained Mike, telling him that Mr. Marshall had called to find out if they had returned from the reservation.

"He asked to talk with you, Mike. He said it was important," she said with concern.

"Now, what the hell could he want? Maybe he wants to put me into one of those plays of his. Maybe he thinks all us Montagnes can sing and dance like Joey," he sneered.

Lily looked him straight in the eyes. "It's about the Center. It's been wrecked. I think he needs your help."

When Joey heard the news, tired as he was from the ride, he called Birdie and they decided to walk over to the

Center to see what damage had been done. Before he left the house, Lily told him how depressed Jim Marshall had sounded on the phone, and that Mike had not called back, telling her that it could wait until the next day, that he was going to The Longhouse.

As they approached the store, they could see the wooden barriers that had been placed around the entrance. A single police car was parked out in front. The sidewalk was still littered with the remains of the front windows, swept into neat piles against the walls of the building. The orange curtains lay torn and twisted, like the downed banners of some defeated army. Red and yellow paint smears ran from the doorway down the length of the store and up onto the walls, like a weird modern painting that had no beginning or end. On the walls someone had scrawled huge four-letter obscenities that scorned the Center and the people who came to it. The tables had been overturned, as well as the bookcases and the portable blackboard. The travel posters were in shreds, slashed by a sharp instrument or the hands of the sick and angry invaders.

Jim and Thora Marshall, dressed in dungarees, were inside, talking to two policemen, as Joey and Birdie entered.

"It's a dirty shame," one of the cops was saying.

"Punks . . . that's what they are, lowdown sneaks who don't give a darn about anything or anybody. There sure are enough of them around these days, and I'm afraid we are too easy on them. I'd personally like to catch the rats responsible for this," the second one added as he closed his pad, having written some notes given to him by Marshall.

Thora was standing behind her husband, a broom in her hand.

"So that's how it is, officer." She greeted Joey and Birdie. "Hi, kids. Welcome to the ruins. For the fine sum of a quarter—twenty-five cents—I'll give you a personal guided tour."

She threw the broom down in disgust.

"How awful! It seems impossible that anyone would do a thing like this," Birdie said.

"Oh it's possible, all right," one of the cops said. "You just come with us on a tour of night duty and you'll see enough stuff to turn your stomach."

"But why?" Joey asked. "Why, Mr. Marshall?"

"Beats me, Joey. I thought we were being friendly, trying to help them out. Can you imagine what they'd do to their real enemies?"

"Jim, I just can't get you to understand. To them, whoever they are, *we* are their enemies," Thora Marshall said.

"Well, we've got to get back to the station," a policeman said. "I guess you'll be hearing from the detective division."

"Thanks, gentlemen, for your sympathy," Thora told them, wondering why the destruction of the Center could take place so silently and swiftly as to go undetected by cruising police cars.

When they had left, Marshall said, "Now, don't go getting bitter about them, Thora. They've got their hands full as it is."

"Full of what?" she said angrily.

"How did it happen, Mr. Marshall? When did you find out about it?" Joey asked anxiously.

"Maybe they're tired of talking about it, Joey," Birdie said.

"Oh, one more time won't hurt. And if anyone deserves an explanation, you kids do," Marshall answered.

Mrs. Marshall began. "We'd just stepped out to the candy store for a few minutes last night at about ten o'clock. Jim had a headache and I thought I could get him a bromo seltzer. The place had been dead, except for a Lebanese waiter from one of the restaurants on Atlantic Avenue. Someone told him he could get help with his preparation for his citizenship exam. We reviewed some American history, and he left. Jim suggested that we call it a night and that we both go to the candy store."

Marshall picked up. "There I was, head splitting wide open, and me sitting and sipping my bromo like it was champagne, when we hear a terrific crashing of glass. We thought it might have been an auto accident, so we ran to the street to look. We couldn't see any cars down this way . . . but there, in the moonlight, the splintered glass glittered like it was Santa's workshop in Macy's window. We ran like crazy, even forgot to pay the candy store man. And there it was . . . the demilitarized zone, right here in Brooklyn."

"Well," Mrs. Marshall asked them, "how do you like our ever-growing popularity? They're just breaking the door down, trying to get in."

"Honey, that's enough. You keep that up, you'll be joining the ulcer club," Marshall warned.

"We came down tonight, thinking we could start the clean-up but the police tell us that since the Center is tied into possible federal funds, we shouldn't touch a thing until the detectives take pictures and do a report. It seems like J. Edgar Hoover might pay us a visit, in person," Mrs. Marshall explained.

"He doesn't know we exist . . . or maybe I should use the past tense—existed. Gosh, that sounds so final," said Marshall.

"We still exist, Jim. It may not look like much right now, but we exist," his wife told him.

"It was a rotten thing to do, Mr. Marshall. Do you have any idea who's responsible?" Joey asked.

"Not the slightest, Joey. I don't imagine it was any of the afternoon kids; they're too young and scared to do a thing like that. But it might be some of the older boys— our evening clientele. And if they didn't like what we were trying to do for them, couldn't they have come out and told us about it, instead of huffing and puffing and trying to blow the house down?"

Thora Marshall lit a cigarette. Her nervousness was evident.

"Jim, I hate to oversimplify, but here's the way I see it. This little place is like a beacon in the night. It stands out like a sore thumb. And it's not a bar, or a poolroom, and it's not a church. It's . . . it's like some strange blotch on someone's body. You don't know how it got there. It's just there, and so you begin to scratch it, pick at it, and worry it, hoping it'll go away—anything that will relieve your discomfort. This little place represents school, teachers, books, education—in short, it's everything that frustrates so many of the kids. It reminds them of someone prying into their discontentment with themselves, with society. When you want to show how much you hate authority, you want to shove your fist in its face. Well, they don't mean to hurt you, personally. They just don't see any reason for going to school—*any* kind of school, including this poor little excuse-of-a-place which is trying to get them back to earning that diploma."

Jim sounded utterly resigned as he spoke. "I'm about ready to give up, Thora. I don't know if I can take any more. It makes me feel foolish to sit here and say 'Step right up, boys and girls, get your red-hot diplomas. Just keep on coming back here and we'll see that you get it.'"

"Feeling a little foolish never really hurt anybody, Jim. Maybe it's good for your ego, once in a while. And just think of what might happen if you'll only stick it out—if you show them you've got the time and patience to wait for them, in spite of the broken windows, the paint, the maliciousness."

"I guess you're right, Thora. Come to think of it, you're always right."

"Not always, Jim. Just most of the time. You'd hate to be married to someone who's always right."

"Right again, honey." Marshall smiled.

Birdie loved listening to the Marshalls, the smooth flow of their relationship. She hoped that when she and Joey married, they might find the same harmony of softness and strength that made the Marshalls so enviable.

"Mr. Marshall, I know you're waiting to hear from my uncle, and if I can make a suggestion—"

"Sure, Joey, go ahead."

"I assume you want to talk to him about the Center. Forget doing it on the phone. He's down at The Longhouse. I've got a hunch this is the time to do it, and the bar is the right place. In front of the other guys, he might be ashamed to say no."

"Joey, you make it sound like that great scene in *High*

Noon, you know, where they face each other on the main street, holster to holster, heart-beat to heart-beat." Marshall smiled.

"Joey's right, Jim. You ought to get his uncle right where it hurts," Mrs. Marshall agreed, reaching for the broom.

"Where are you going with that?" Marshall asked.

"Oh, I just thought I might take it along, to pick up the pieces, whomever they belong to."

"You are going home, right now! And so are these kids. When the Lone Ranger rides, he rides alone. But one thing I will ask, honey. Since I never did finish that bromo last night, you might just have a long, cool one ready when I get home. My head may be in for some fancy bumps from Mr. Montagne and friends."

"Are you sure you wouldn't like me to go along?" Mrs. Marshall asked.

"Woman's place is in the home. After The Longhouse I'll want someone nice to come home to, I'm sure."

"Do you hear that, kids? I think he means me. At least, I'm the only other Marshall in his home."

The Marshalls linked arms, and walked to the door of the Center.

"They say imitation is one of the best ways to learn something," Joey whispered to Birdie, "so, baby, let's have your arm."

As they followed the Marshalls to the street, they noticed people walking by the Center, not paying attention to the barriers or the glass, not aware of the importance of the wrecked store, and the part it was playing in welding the strong friendship between themselves and Jim and Thora Marshall.

*   *   *

Jim Marshall arrived at The Longhouse to find the place crowded, filled with the haze of smoke, and the particular odor of hops and malt, common to most bars. Men were sitting in booths, or standing at the bar, talking loudly, laughing, trying to hear each other above the noise.

As he stood in the doorway, dozens of eyes turned in his direction. Few strangers ever visited The Longhouse; it was more like a private club, limited to its ironworker membership. He walked to the bar and ordered a bottle of Ballantine. He looked around casually. There was Mike sitting at one of the tables. Marshall carried his bottle over to Mike's table and bent forward to greet him. Mike was busy talking to another man and hadn't seen Marshall approach.

"Good evening, Mr. Montagne. I'm Marshall, Joey's teacher."

The men had stopped their conversation. They waited and listened.

Mike looked up, took a slow swallow of beer. He looked Marshall over, lifted his bottle again, wiped his mouth with the back of his hand.

"Oh, I know who you are. But, you're not lookin' for Joey in here, are ya?" His voice sounded cold and clear, ready for combat.

The men chuckled.

"No. As a matter of fact, I just left him a few minutes ago. No, Mr. Montagne, I'm here to see *you*—if you can spare me a few minutes."

"Sure, why not. Any friend of Joey's is a frienda mine." Mike spoke the words with stabbing sarcasm. "What can I do for you?"

"I'd rather speak to you alone, if you don't mind."

"They're okay," he said, pointing to the others. "Whatever y'got to say, you can say it to all of us."

Marshall hesitated, took a quick swig at the bottle, when he noticed the men were drinking in that manner. He felt ill-at-ease and uncomfortable standing there, but there was no space to sit at the table, and nobody offered him a seat.

"Friendly bunch," he said to himself, and took a deep breath to bolster his courage.

"Mr. Montagne, I need your help . . . *we* need your help."

"*My* help? You—we . . . What's it all about?" Mike pulled himself up, like a judge trying to impress the courtroom.

Marshall told him about the Center—how the tutorial program was failing in its attempts to attract dropouts who could be bolstered in their work and prepared to graduate from high school. He went on to tell those at the table about the vandalism—and of his own discouragement.

"Frankly, Mr. Montagne, we need some backing from all the parents—from the community, too. I've talked to Father Bello at St. Paul's and he promised to cooperate by mentioning it at services. He's even offered the social hall for a meeting, so we can explain to the kids who've dropped out, and their parents, how the Center can help them. Otherwise, I'm afraid it's going to mean tossing in the towel. We can't keep the Center open if it doesn't show results. That's why I'm here."

"What're ya tellin' *me* this for? I got no kids. I've got nothin' to do with your Center," Mike replied defensively.

"That's just it, Mr. Montagne. Nobody—that is, few parents—are aware of what we're trying to do. We sent some leaflets home, but I'm not sure they were ever delivered, or ever read. That didn't help much. But if you'd help us by organizing a meeting, or pushing the idea among your fellow steelworkers, maybe then we'd stand a chance."

"First of all, Marshall," Mike sneered, "we're not steelworkers. We call ourselves ironworkers—boomers. People who don't know any better call us steelworkers."

"I'm sorry, Mr. Montagne," Marshall was quick to apologize. "I stand corrected. A teacher is always willing to learn something new."

His soft words broke the tension; the men smiled and let Marshall know that they had liked his honesty.

"I don't know nothin' about organizin' meetings. I wouldn't know where to start," Mike protested.

"If you could get the Union to put out a notice, I'll handle St. Paul's with Father Bello, and the art department at the high school will make up some posters we can put in stores around the neighborhood." Marshall's enthusiasm was running high. "If we can get enough people to come and hear what we want to tell them, Mr. Montagne, you might keep the Center alive. That's all I ask—the chance to keep it going!"

Mike sat there, contemplating his drink. The men spoke up in a flurry of words, urging Mike to take the lead.

"C'mon, Mike! The guy ain't askin' too much."

"We'll help ya!"

Mike raised his palms; the others fell silent. "I'd like to think it over for a few minutes, if ya don't mind." He looked up, riveting his eyes on Marshall.

"How come you're so interested in our neighborhood, Marshall? You don't even live here."

"It's a long story, Mr. Montagne. If you don't mind, I'll give you the short version. I grew up in Harlem. My father was a Pullman porter and he worked his heart out supporting his wife and six kids. I was the youngest, and after he saw his oldest son quit school and become a problem, he swore that the rest of us would finish. I remember him telling me once, 'Jimmy, I don't want you being a porter like your old man, or a bum like your brother. I'm going to see to it that you get the best education me and the good Lord'll allow. You're going to go all the way, up and through college. And, when you stand there, with your diploma in your hand, I pray me and your mom are around to shake your hand. Someday, Jimmy, you take all them books and ideas—all that education—and give it back to your folks—or anyone what needs it.' " The memory was still vivid, although Jim had been unaware it was all there, waiting to be shared.

The men were silent, catching every word between swallows from their glasses or bottles.

Marshall went on. "My dad never saw that day, Mr. Montagne. He died before I graduated. But when I decided I wanted to become a teacher, I was thinking of him, not only of myself. And I knew he'd be glad and proud—for me, for himself."

"How come you don't wanna work with your own people?" Mike inquired.

"I guess I've never thought of any one group as being my own. When people are in trouble, I don't see them as black, pink, or polka-dotted—just people who need help, and if I can help out, I like to do so. I teach a lot of kids from this neighborhood, and I've gotten to know about their problems. I'm sure there are white teachers who feel exactly the same way about kids in Harlem. It's not all black or all white. The trouble is, there never seems to be enough people to help when and where it's needed. The Center is only another way of trying to get help to the kids, Mr. Montagne, to keep them from lousing up any chance they may have at getting a decent life for themselves."

"I never been to college, Marshall, an' my life ain't so bad," Mike boasted.

"The world's different nowadays, Mr. Montagne. It isn't only the diploma that guarantees a good life—it's the idea that a youngster has self-respect, that he doesn't feel defeated by a society in which he hasn't even begun to function." Marshall wondered if he was talking above them.

Mike looked around the table at the others, who looked back at him, waiting for his reaction.

"That's a very touchin' story ya got there, Marshall. But you know somethin'. We've all got touchin' stories. I bet you don't have enough time to listen to my own, or Pete's here, or John's, or a hundred other boomers I could introduce ya to. And we didn't have any teachers worryin' about us. When we got out of school, we went right to work, and we've been workin' ever since. It does a kid good to get knocked around a little. It gives him some muscle. Kids have got too many people worryin' about them these days—people who should mind their own business." He sounded proud of his response, as though being a spokesman for the group could only elevate him in their eyes.

"But, Mr. Montagne, kids *are* my business. I would like . . ."

"Marshall, I ain't finished yet." Mike placed his empty bottle in front of him, pulled a cigar out of his shirt pocket, chewed off the end, lighted it, and drew a slow, strong puff.

"Livin' in this neighborhood may be tough, but we like it that way. We take care of our problems the best way we know how. And if you ask me, we ain't doin' such a bad job. Maybe you better stick to puttin' on them plays of yours. You say kids are your business. I don't see where you've done such a good job with Joey, puttin' ideas in his head that don't belong there. Maybe it gets down to this, Marshall. *Our* kids are *our* business . . . and you just don't belong."

The last few words were drowned by the murmurs of approval of the men sitting near Mike.

"You're right, Mike. Tell him off."

"Give him hell, Mike!"

"Attaboy!"

Each response was like a stinging blow across Marshall's face. He had known that talking with Mike Montagne was not going to be easy, but he had not expected Mike's bitterness about Joey to blind him to the idea that he might be of help in saving the Center.

"Well, gentlemen, what can I say? I came to you for help. Maybe that's a sign of weakness to you. I just don't happen to look at it that way. You know, maybe you fellows have been up too high and too long—up there on the beams. It's a pretty rare atmosphere, and it probably breeds conditions of its own, a way of thinking and a way of looking at life that's different from us weak, little ants on the ground. I'll tell you this. Something a lot of you may have learned at school long ago. What goes up must come down. Maybe one of these days you'll see that you're wrong, that you're up in the clouds in more ways than one.

But you'll find out that it's too late—too late for your kids and too late for yourselves. In your own language, gentlemen, you are giving your kids the royal shaft. I guess that's all I can say right now. You've won, and I hope it makes you very happy."

The men sat in stunned silence, not knowing how to react. Marshall walked to the door, looked up at the sign that hung over it, turned to where Mike sat and said, "Don't you believe it!"

12

THE NEXT AFTERNOON, after a routine day at school, Joey was sitting in the office of the school newspaper, *Prospects,* typing an editorial he had been thinking about for the next issue.

He had talked with Arthur Simon, the editor-in-chief, about the possibility of submitting a guest editorial about the Center and the tutoring program. Simon thought it was a good idea but told Joey he would have to work fast because the next issue of the newspaper would be going to press before the end of the week.

Mr. Marshall had asked him to remain after English class and told him about Mike's refusal to have anything to do with the Center. Joey was not surprised, but he felt a keen frustration at not knowing what to do next, a feeling he knew he shared with the Marshalls and Birdie. Maybe the school paper, he thought . . . an editorial.

The idea for the editorial came to him in a dream, and he was anxious to put it down before it escaped him. In his dream, he was one of the young men standing around a divan on which Socrates lay, half-reclining, with a cup of hemlock in his hand, sipping the poisonous brew which would take him to his dignified death. As Socrates lifted the cup, Joey saw that the face was that of Mr. Marshall. He tried to stop his teacher from drinking but was restrained in the tight grip of two of the philosopher's other disciples. When Joey awoke, he untangled the symbolism of the dream, knowing that it was a strange blend of an illustration he had seen in a history textbook and the events that had occurred at the Center.

He watched the words emerge from the typewriter:

> They say the populace of Athens stoned Socrates on his way to his home after his trial at the foot of the Acropolis. That old man, probably one of the world's greatest teachers in his time, had been blamed for corrupting the youth of his beloved city!
>
> What the people of that time believed were dangerous ideas are the same ideas by which many of today's democracies exist. A teacher of Athens had tried to do his job, to open minds, to prepare them for a good life in the future. How was he rewarded? He was vilified and put to death! The only blame we can place with Socrates is that he put too much faith in the intelligence of his fellow Athenians! What he thought was courage turned out to be stupidity. For if it takes courage to *learn*, it takes *guts* to shake off the shackles of ignorance!

Joey was aware of someone behind him, peering over his shoulder. It was Marshall.

"Nice going, Joey! What a good idea to draw a parallel between ancient Greece and Brooklyn. But I'm afraid it's a shot in the dark. We're going to need much more than an editorial to shake things up. And I mean fast. My wife tells me the detectives called her office to tell her that they did all they had to at the Center, and that it's got to be boarded up indefinitely—something about it being unsafe for occupants. She phoned Father Bello, and he said we could use the social hall at St. Paul's until we get the store fixed again. *Tempus fugit,* as your Roman friends might say."

"You mean Greek friends, don't you?"

"If I knew how to say it in Greek I would have, Joey. There are limits to what even an English teacher knows," he smiled.

"How would we go about getting the store fixed, Mr. Marshall?"

"I don't really know, Joey. And frankly, I've begun to think that it may not be worth it. The punks who visited it the other night could probably do it again, and I don't really have time to play those kind of games."

"I know what you mean," Joey said.

Birdie bounced into the office, slamming the door jubilantly.

"I thought I might find you both here. Stay put. Don't move. In fact, maybe you'd better sit down. This just might be the idea of the century." Her eyes glowed with enthusiasm.

"It's just what we need," Joey answered, "one good idea."

"Well, ever since I heard about Mike's big fat no to Mr. Marshall, I was wondering where we might go, who we might approach next—that is, if we still agree on the idea that we need the neighborhood's help."

"We still do, Birdie," Marshall confirmed.

"I don't know if you're ready for this. In my research for my project, I did quite a bit of reading about Iroquois culture, and of course, that includes the Mohawks. It seems that women were pretty important—not the way they are in our society, but as leaders in government and religion and family life. Wait a minute . . . here, I jotted it down directly from a book. 'The Iroquois woman was no downtrodden drudge. There is no question but at the time of the European contact, the Iroquois woman occupied a higher, freer, and more influential place in her society than did the European woman in hers. In the longhouse and in the clearing, the Iroquois woman's position was securely based on her leadership in the family and in agriculture.' "

She paused to catch her breath. "So, gentlemen, next we go to Lily, and my mother, and all the Caughnawaga women. If the men won't have anything to do with saving the Center, we women will!"

Marshall and Joey were smiling, not as though they were amused, but rather with a sense of relief that maybe Birdie had hit on a way to pick up the pieces.

"Mr. Marshall, I'd like your wife's help," Birdie continued. "I think we ought to call a meeting. Maybe at St. Paul's. Maybe at the Union Hall on Atlantic Avenue. Somewhere. We've got to get the mothers and sisters and aunts of those kids busy with the responsibility that their fathers and brothers and uncles have ignored. What do you think?"

"It's worth a try," Marshall said.

"Birdie, I think it's absolutely brilliant," Joey beamed.

"It's not brilliant if it doesn't work. But I'd like to see us try, anyway."

Marshall reached into his pocket. "Birdie, here's a dime, and my wife's office number. That's what I've heard said

. . . behind every good woman, stands a man." They laughed.

The three of them walked as fast as they could, down the long hall to the public telephone.

A week later the old Union Hall on Atlantic Avenue was filled to its usual capacity for a regular weekly business meeting. Tonight, though, there was one difference. The ironworkers had brought along their wives, as they had been instructed to do in a bulletin received in the mail. The main speaker, it had announced, would be a Mrs. James Marshall, although the topic of her address was only explained as being of prime importance to the parents of the community.

The hall buzzed with expectancy. Who was the impressive-looking black couple sitting near Sam Simpson, the Union business agent, who usually chaired the meetings? And why was Father Bello sitting between Lily Montagne and Birdie Le Brun?

Sam glanced at his watch, nodded to the others on the platform, rose, and approached the lectern. A slow hush fell over the audience.

"Brothers—" the voice was strong—"and I guess I might as well say, sisters . . . although I've never heard it said from this platform before. We are going to postpone the regular business until after our special speaker. You might say we turned you into a captive audience this way, but we think our speaker has some very important things to say, things that concern many of you, and we didn't want you walking out before she had a chance to talk with you.

"Some of us are under the impression that a Union exists only for Union business. If you believe that, you're wrong. We've been here on Atlantic Avenue a good number of years now, and we've seen the neighborhood change and grow as we changed and grew. We are interested in what happens in Gowanus and Boerum Hill and Brooklyn Heights and Borough Hall. Now, that's a pretty big chunk of territory, with a pretty mixed population, and at least a dozen problems I could tell you about that need immediate attention.

"The lady sitting up here tonight is a social worker. And she's got herself involved in one of our problems, even though she doesn't live in the neighborhood. She needs your help. I'd like you to listen to her carefully, and then each of you out there—not *only* the women—figure out what you can do to help her. I've got a strong feeling that by helping her, you're going to help yourselves." He turned toward Thora Marshall. "Mrs. Marshall, they're all yours."

Thora Marshall rose from her seat. The audience had buzzed after Sam Simpson's introduction, and the sounds made her slightly tense. She walked to the lectern, looked out at the audience, and smiled warmly.

"Good evening. Mr. Simpson referred to you as brothers and sisters, and if you'll allow me to, I'd like to think of you that way.

"I really appreciate this opportunity to tell you about some of your youngsters, and what some of them are doing—or not doing—that may easily affect their futures and yours.

"Some of you may have seen me in the neighborhood. I've been spending quite a bit of time at that old store on Atlantic Avenue, a few blocks from here. I don't think of it as just a store, but rather what we've tried to change it into—a Neighborhood Center, where you could come with your problems and possibly find answers to them."

Her eyes pierced the audience. "Would you raise your hands in response to these questions, please. How many of you have used the Center for day care . . . you know, a place where women can leave their preschool children while they work part-time?"

She scanned the large room. "I see three hands. Thank you."

A tide of soft whispers rose and swept through the hall.

"How many of the senior citizens in your families have come down to the Center to use its facilities, to just sit and talk, or play cards, or read magazines . . . or more importantly, to talk with Father Bello or myself about your social security benefits, or health problems?" She saw the sprinkling of hands. "Seven . . . well, we're getting better. Thank you."

Buzzing. Whispering. Buzzing.

"How many of your sons and daughters, who are having problems in the junior or senior high schools they attend have you sent to us?"

Buzzing. Whispering. Hesitation. No hands raised.

"No, no, ladies and gentlemen, I don't mean how many have the schools sent us. I have in my hand a list of more than thirty names given us by the schools, with the hope that your youngsters would take advantage of the help we can offer. So far, we have seen about ten. The school can only recommend that your kids come. It's up to you to see that they do.

"If this sounds like a sales pitch, forgive it, please. The teachers who are there at the Center, who want to help, are giving their time freely, as volunteers . . . and so am I."

The hall seemed to quiet down suddenly. Her voice probed the silence.

"About a week ago, the Center was practically destroyed. We don't know who did it, but we have a pretty good idea. Whoever did the damage, did it out of anger. The store itself doesn't really matter, because we can find another place, if we have to. What does matter is that there are young people against the *idea* of the Center, and angry enough to keep it from coming to life . . . from doing the job it can do . . . angry enough to keep my husband and me from doing our jobs." She turned toward where Jim Marshall sat.

"I'm not used to talking this loud or this long, so I'm going to let my husband take over . . . but I'll be back."

She turned and walked to her seat, passing Marshall on the way. Jim Marshall stood where she had stood, raised his head and let his deep voice resound through the room.

"Maybe some of you don't know what my job is. My job in that Center is to help some of your sons tackle the schoolwork which has defeated them, which has made them drop out. We'd like to see them finish high school—not just to attend a graduation ceremony, not only so they can hold a diploma in their hands! There are lessons to be learned at the study Center—lessons that go far beyond simple problems in mathematics and science and English. The *most* important lesson is one I know many of you have learned on your jobs—up on the beams. What is that lesson? It deals with how to accept a challenge, how to conquer your frustrations so you can accomplish the goal you've set for yourself. Having that diploma doesn't guarantee that your son will become a good man, but the discipline involved can give him a feeling of accomplishment and confidence, a sense of the positive, which many young people seem to lack today.

"I don't know how long it'll take for the study Center to get back on its feet, but I know that the store itself must *not* stay empty. If that store dies, it'll be like some of the things you men out there have erected—if they were standing empty and unused! Wouldn't that be a waste of human effort if your work wasn't being put to some use? It's *people* who make bridges and buildings come alive! And that's all I'm asking for. A chance to make that study Center work and come alive—a chance to put some of your youngsters back on the right track.

"If any of you have questions or want to speak up, I'll be glad to hear from you. Thank you for listening."

To most of the audience, this news about the Center—what it was, and how it had been vandalized—was the first news they had heard. A small ripple of shock went through the crowd as husbands and wives conferred, as neighbor turned to neighbor in bewilderment.

Jim Marshall, sitting once again in his seat, noticed an elderly man near the center of the hall. His thin hand went up like a banner.

Jim went forward again to the edge of the platform.

"Yes, sir," he said, pointing and signaling the old man to rise.

The man stood, hat in hand.

"I'm Jonas Crowfoot, age seventy-six, retired, and with a lotta time on my hands. I get to see a lot of what goes on in the neighborhood, and I can tell you this, things *have* changed—and not for the better! Seems like all the young people nowadays is interested in is *big* things, *fast* things, *expensive* things! I was among the first group of Indians to come down this way to work and live. Things was more simple then. We just worried about doin' a good day's work and giving our families the best life we could. But now? Now it's all changed. Today it's who's got the biggest, fastest car? Who can drink the most?

"We worked long and hard to buy some of these houses in the neighborhood, and we used to keep 'em looking good. I think when we Indians started livin' like the white man, we lost a lot of the good Indian customs we brought with us from Canada. Good things, like strong family feelings and feelin' proud of a good job done with your hands. I'd like to see some of our young people forget the money and remember some of that fine Caughnawaga blood that, I hope, is still runnin' in their veins! I'm not an educated man, but I wished many, many times I could read 'n write better'n I can now, and maybe understand more of this crazy world. I can still work with my hands—so, if I can offer a couple hours help a day, down there at your store, I'd be glad to. And my missus is great with a broom and mop. I'm sure she'll want to join me."

The old man's offer brought a smattering of applause.

"Thank you, Mr. Crowfoot. I accept your offer."

A woman toward the rear of the hall raised her hand for recognition.

"My name is Michelle Reilly. My friends call me Mickey. I'm Caughnawaga and my husband . . . well you know what my husband is with a name like Reilly. Our son's not been doing too good in school, at least if I can judge from those red marks on his report card. We've never heard about getting him help at that Center of yours. But you can bet your boots, he'll be seeing you as soon as you tell me where I send him. I'm just a housewife, and I don't know what I can do to help. But you just let me know, and I'll be glad to help."

Thora Marshall was standing at her husband's side. She addressed the group. "Thank you, Mrs. Reilly. Ladies and gentlemen, we don't want to take too much of your evening, so with Mr. Simpson's permission, and with Father Bello's gracious invitation, the ladies are now invited to the social hall at St. Paul's, to continue our portion of the meeting."

Noise filled the hall, chairs being shuffled, people talking excitedly as a number of the women headed toward the doorway. On the platform, the Marshalls and Lily and Birdie were shaking hands with Sam Simpson and Father Bello. The women walked off the platform with Father Bello and Jim Marshall.

In the front row, where Joey sat with Papa Montagne and Mike, some of Mike's friends sat silently, waiting for his reaction.

He stood, and stretched, like a huge bear coming out of hibernation.

"I never thought I'd see the day when women would take over the Union Hall," he told them.

"They haven't taken over, Mike," Joey said defensively.

"What are you waitin' for, kid? Ain't you headed for St. Paul's? Seems to me you belong there more than you do here," Mike snapped.

"The boy belongs wherever he feels like, Mike," Papa said, "wherever he feels his friends are. Come on, Joey, I'll walk with you."

Outside the hall there were clusters of women, gathering in groups for the walk to St. Paul's.

Birdie and Lily approached Joey. Lily said, "Joey, isn't your grandfather staying for the rest of the meeting?"

Papa overheard her. "What for, Lily? It's the same old stuff. Why tonight's been the most exciting thing that's happened in that old hall since the last strike call, a couple of years ago."

"Did you really think so, Papa?" Birdie asked.

"Cross my heart, Birdie."

"I think the Marshalls were wonderful," Birdie said.

"That's something you and I knew long ago, Birdie," Joey answered.

"Well, we're going over to St. Paul's, Joey. Mrs. Marshall has asked me to help get things organized," Lily said.

"Me too," Birdie added.

"Papa and I will see you later, Mom. Do you want us to come and get you?"

"Don't be silly, Joey," Birdie told him. "You don't have to worry about a couple of dozen women walking through the streets together, no matter how late it is."

"Never thought of it that way," Joey answered.

They separated, going their different ways.

When Papa and Joey arrived home, there was a telegram under the door. The phone was ringing. Joey handed the telegram to Papa and ran to answer the phone.

"Hello."

"Joey, that you? Hal Golding. Hope I didn't scare you with the telegram. I've been trying to reach you every way I know how. I've even got my girl winding up a carrier pigeon. I need your help. One of the Astronauts is in trouble with the police. Possession of marijuana. They won't be able to perform this weekend. Do you think you can step in?"

Papa was shouting from the living room. "Joey, it's for you, from Mr. Golding."

"I know, Papa. I know!"

13

GOLDING'S PHONE CALL had brought confusion along with excitement. Did Joey have a glossy photo they could blow up for out front at The Living End? And for publicity? No. Well, it wasn't important. They would do a quick hand-painted poster, and releases would be sent to the city newspapers announcing the substitution. Did Joey have a special costume he would wear? No. How about one of those white ruffled-front shirts, with ruffled sleeves and a tight-fitting pair of black trousers? No shirt like that? Pick up one at one of the mod boutiques in the Village on the way over. Black boots? Yes, Joey had those. Could you tie some red streamers onto the guitar. Why? Just a bit of color to add to the stark quality of only black and white. Birdie could do that. What time for showing up at The Living End? Three hours before show time, for a run-through, at five o'clock. Bring your family along as our guests. Got it all straight, Joey? See you soon. Click.

The hours passed heavily until Saturday afternoon, and after the initial excitement had worn off, Lily and Papa tried not to talk about it with Joey. If he had a need to talk with them, he would. At school he had had to talk about half his classmates out of showing up at The Living End on Saturday night. He was pleased and flattered by the response of his friends in the Plays and Players, and on *Prospects*, and the kids in his classes, and many of the teachers, and the basketball team wanting to show en masse. It was too much, and he didn't want to risk being more nervous than he should be. An audience of friends and neighbors and classmates and relatives would never allow him to measure his performance objectively. It would not be fair to him, nor to Golding, to have his first audiences neatly wrapped, tied with a bow, and delivered like the canned laughter he hated on television.

Saturday afternoon. Three o'clock. Joey sat on the edge of his bed, rehearsing his songs. He was pleased with the way his voice sounded and with the sureness with which his fingers moved across the guitar strings. Birdie had bought some red ribbon at the five-and-ten, cut it into short and long streamers which hung gracefully from the guitar. They did add something—Golding knew his business—but Joey wanted to get used to them, to see that they did not distract him. He stood and tried a song from that position. He had not thought too much about stage movement before this. Would be stand through all of the songs? Would he sit? Would he move around? Golding would help him, he was sure. He wished he could plan his moves himself, but that would have to wait until he got to The Living End.

On the table near his bed lay the sandwich and glass of milk Lily had brought to his room. He found the food sticking in his throat, so he abandoned the sandwich after a few small bites. The milk he gulped down in great swallows.

What had he read in a magazine once about Tallulah Bankhead . . . before a performance she ate nothing . . . after, a dozen of the best oysters and a bottle of champagne. The private rituals of famous performers were always fascinating, and he wondered whether he might one day find his own.

He packed his guitar carefully in its case, folding the ribbons over gently so they would not be creased.

Three-thirty. He washed his face with cool water, patted it dry and contemplated himself in the bathroom mirror. He hoped he would not need to wear make-up. That would depend on the lighting, and Golding's advice. He walked to the closet and removed his black trousers, leaving them on the hanger, wrapped in plastic.

As he opened his bedroom door, he heard Birdie's voice at the bottom of the stairs, talking with Lily and Papa, going over the directions on how to get to The Living End.

Birdie was not sure whether Lily and Papa would be coming by subway until Papa told her Mike was driving them in, even if Papa had to pay for parking. So Mike would be coming too. She was glad in a way. It was better to have him there, even grudgingly, than absent, with all the tension that would follow his not being there.

Joey and Birdie said good-bye and walked toward the subway. He carried his guitar case, she, the trousers. On Eighth Street, they saw the shirt Golding had described in the window of the Village Esquire. Joey tried it on, and it looked fine, so he bought it, asking them not to wrap it up but to put it on the trouser hanger instead. Twelve dollars, which Golding had told Joey he would be glad to reimburse. On the way to Bleecker Street, they paused to look at a record shop window. Cascading from left to right were all the latest hit albums . . . the Beatles, Sonny and Cher, Harry Belafonte, faces or weird artistic designs to attract and please the millions of young people all over the world who were their fans. They looked at each other, and smiled, silently sharing the same thought, the same hope. Those names had started somewhere, facing their first audiences in Liverpool or California, or Trinidad. They had made their mark, with hard work, and patience, and luck, and the loyalty of their fans, and the talent that made each of them unique and memorable.

Maybe . . . maybe.

Birdie broke the silence as they turned down MacDougall Street.

"Do you think they'll mind my being there with you . . . so early?"

"Not at all. At least, I don't think Golding will mind," Joey said.

"I hope not. I'll stay out of your way," she said.

"You'd never get in my way. I might as well start with one good friend around. I'm going to need every friend I can find tonight."

Birdie had never heard Joey refer to her as friend before, and she liked the way he had said it, as though he had taken an often abused word, and given it fresh, new meaning.

A few minutes later, and they were standing outside The Living End. Large black letters on a poster announced the name: Lonny Arlen. In smaller letters, below, were printed the words:

EXTRA ATTRACTION
Joey Montagne
The Singing Mohawk

Joey was furious. Golding had said something about a poster. But not The Singing Mohawk. Not that!

Birdie saw his angry look. "What's wrong, Joey?"

"Look at that, will you?"

"I still don't see what's wrong?"

"Birdie Le Brun, don't you go getting me angry, too!"

He went toward the poster, and Birdie thought he was about to rip it from the frame.

"I don't want to be known as a 'Singing Mohawk!' I just want to be a good entertainer. Do they bill Tony Bennett as the Singing Italian, or Sidney Poitier as the Acting Negro?!" The image of the Seminoles flashed across his mind.

"Don't you see, Birdie, this makes me some kind of freak! They'll expect me to come out in moccasins, carrying a tom-tom and then go into my rain dance! Or maybe they expect me to wear a feather headdress down to my knees. That's not what I want!"

"Gee, Joey, I never thought about it that way. We're proud of being Caughnawagas. I can't see any harm in letting anyone know about it."

"Not this way, Birdie. It's cheap—like a sideshow act in a carnival. I don't mind anyone knowing about my Indian blood, but first I'd like to show them I can sing, that I have myself to offer—not some novelty, some gimmick."

"Joey, don't say anything until after tonight. I don't think it's a good idea. Besides, I'm sure Golding didn't mean any harm. Wait—you can tell him about it later."

"Maybe you're right, Birdie. But just wait 'til after I'm finished. I'll give him a piece of my Indian mind!"

They entered the coffeehouse, empty now except for two waitresses who were busy behind the counter, getting huge urns of coffee ready. A large espresso machine gleamed in the dim light, and under a canopy of Plexiglass on the countertop and in display cases were a varied assortment of pastries and cakes, looking like a patchwork quilt.

Joey asked for Hal Golding and was directed to the dressing rooms in the rear, behind a huge screen covered with old theatre posters.

Joey knocked at the door and Golding's voice invited them to enter.

"Hello, Mr. Golding, I'd like you to meet my friend, Birdie Le Brun."

"Hello, Birdie. Joey, baby, am I ever so glad to see you! I just got here not five minutes ago myself. Been talking to my lawyer uptown about helping Tom Stone, the Astronaut they caught with the mary jane. Nasty stuff. Too bad it happened. Could ruin them before they really get started. We'll do everything we can to help. It tears me apart when kids jeopardize their futures by acting foolish."

Joey wondered if he should say anything about the poster. Birdie's look scared him away. Instead he asked, "Can we try a run-through, Mr. Golding?"

"Sure, Joey. Champing at the bit, are you? Well, I don't blame you for wanting to get going. And before we get lost in what we're doing in there, I want to tell you how grateful I am for helping me out. I looked through my file, and some acts are on the road, some just not available. I thought that you were due here soon anyway, so why not now? You'll like working with Lonny Arlen." His confidence reached across to Joey, and put him at ease.

"Ready, kids? Follow me."

He guided them into the large room. Birdie asked Golding if she would be intruding if she could watch Joey rehearse.

"You can sit with me, if you'd like to, Birdie. I can yell lighting cues from back there. Why don't you go change, Joey, and make it out here as fast as you can. I'd like you to meet Lonny Arlen. He'll be here in a few minutes."

As Birdie sat with Golding, her eyes growing accustomed to the dim lighting, she realized how really attractive Golding had made his little club.

One wall, opposite the long counter, was canopied in bright red-and-white striped canvas, making that side of the room look like a large, raised porch, with its small tables and chairs.

From the ceiling, Tiffany lamps hung every few feet, a forest of them, glowing softly beneath their stained glass kaleidoscopes. The tables were covered with red-checked cloths, and each table was crowned with a small, potted fern plant.

The performing area was the most unusual, she observed. There was a simple, red-bricked wall on which a designer had hung literally dozens of antique mirrors, all sizes, all colors—gold, black, and some in silver frames. Anyone standing before the wall during a performance would cast dozens of fragmented reflections at those sitting in the audience. It was breath-taking. In the center of the floor, the focal point of the entire room, was a large old-fashioned pot-bellied stove painted stark white. Overhead, a long rack of pin-spots in amber, blue, and pink bathed the area around the stove.

Golding turned to Birdie. "About an hour from now, they'll be swinging from the rafters."

"It's a very good-looking room, Mr. Golding."

"Well, thanks, I think so too. What I like about it the most, Birdie, is that it doesn't detract from the performer. That's an old trick I learned on Madison Avenue. I wasn't always in the coffeehouse business, you know. I used to be an account exec until the stomach started kicking up an ulcer. I had to take a good, hard look at my life, when the doctor told me I was slowly committing suicide.

"As I was saying, I used to be a consultant on packaging. You know, soup, soap flakes. I learned a lot about public taste. The package has got to be simple and attractive. But the product inside has to be something the public wants or, even better, *needs*. Give them a good product, wrapped pretty, and you've got it made.

"When I decided to start my life over, away from the lunacy of Madison Avenue, I knew I'd do what I always wanted to. And this is it. Golding's gift to show biz. I'm making a nice living, and I love every minute of it."

"That's quite a story, Mr. Golding."

"And you know, young lady, it never ends. I keep getting new kids in here all the time. I can't begin to tell you how great it makes me feel to be giving them their first break. Some of them have gone on to better things. Ever seen Lonny Arlen?"

"No, but I've heard about him, and read about him."

"Nice talent, good, soft comedy . . . not that rat-tat-tat old-fashioned kind. He pokes fun at serious things and gets people to laugh at 'em. There he is now. Hey, Lonny! Come here a minute."

Nice-looking, collegiate type guy, Birdie thought, as the comic made his way to their table.

Golding introduced Birdie and said to Lonny, "Sit down. Joey Montagne'll be out in a minute. I'd like you to let me know what you think."

"Sure thing," said Arlen.

Almost on cue, Joey emerged from behind the curtain screen. Birdie had no idea what the others thought. She only knew that he looked very handsome, almost like a portrait she'd once seen at the Metropolitan Museum of Art. It started out with his black hair, which he had brushed until it shone softly. His eyes looked like luminous, large black buttons; his skin seemed amber in the soft light, and his full mouth opened into a dazzling smile. The simplicity of the white shirt and the coal-black trousers was given added elegance by the brilliant red silk streamers she had tied to the guitar.

Golding beckoned. "Over there, Joey—right alongside the stove."

Joey walked to the place indicated by the voice.

"Okay." Golding yelled over his shoulder, "Johnny, let's have the white spot!"

A sharp beam of light haloed Joey from hair to toes.

"Okay," Golding instructed. "Bring it down to a pin—just on the face."

Joey's body disappeared in the diminished light. Only the face stood out. Light spilled over onto the surface of the guitar. It was stark, impressive, clean.

"Goya! A painting by Goya, that's who you are, Joey," Golding shouted.

Birdie remembered the handsome Spanish grandees of Goya. That's who the artist had been. She was thrilled with what Golding had accomplished with his knowledge of lighting. He had highlighted Joey's good looks, making him even more impressive.

"Rita," he shouted at one of the waitresses, "get a chair and put it out there, on his right!"

A quick scurrying sound, and a chair was in its place.

"All right, Joey, let's see how it looks when you sit and you, Johnny, give me a circle of blue on that floor—around the chair!"

"Great," said Arlen, "the kid looks great!"

"You betcha' life, Lonny. It's the Golding touch." He was kidding, but his pride was evident.

"I'd say his parents had something to do with it," joked Arlen.

Birdie liked these men. She wished Lily and Papa and Mike would come, and her own family and the Marshalls. She was bursting with pride and wanted to share it with someone.

While the others were arranging some further changes in Joey's setup, Birdie wondered about Golding's use of the words "The Singing Mohawk" and whether or not she should try to dissuade Joey from complaining about it until he had thought about it for a few days. Anyone could see that Golding wasn't trying to present Joey to the public as his token Indian. He seemed to want to present him as a talented performer, showing him off to the best advantage.

Everything was ready.

"Okay, Joey, how about a number now? Let's have a standard, then you can switch from standing to sitting, or whatever you like, and then you can do one of your own."

Golding sat down. The waitresses stopped their preparations behind the counter; three bus boys came from the kitchen; even the cashier stood quietly in front of the screen leading to the dressing rooms. Complete silence. Then the soft, sweet sound of Joey's voice floated into the far corners of the room, radiating outward from the central point. The harmony of voice and guitar was perfection; his voice had the freshness of youth which Golding had found in the first audition. He finished the number. The onlookers applauded.

"Cut that!" shouted Golding. "The kid's tryin' to build a mood. You ought to know better than that."

The room quieted. Embarrassed silence.

Slowly, he stood, gracefully lifting one leg so that his foot rested on the seat of the chair. The stance was almost flamenco—classic, elegant.

Joey looked directly at Golding, as he had done during the audition. His voice was confident and clear.

"Ladies and gentlemen. Some of you have forgotten what it's like to be puzzled by your youth and by your innocence. We forget about the ways in which the world separates one generation from another. I'd like to sing a song called 'Fathers and Sons' which speaks for itself."

And, across the darkened room, with only the stark image of his strong face bathed in a sea of blue light, came the words and music of his song.

> We give you laughter;
>   You give us war.
> We give you hope, an occasional tear.
>   You give us days and nights of fear.

We carry schoolbooks;
   You carry guns.
Our games are frightening;
   Your wars are fun.

Each day the distance between us grows.
We look for sunlight, you give us snow.
Just look at these kids, you say,
And you stamp and shout,
Dirty beatniks—they're all way out.
You forget, Mommy and Daddy,
Flappers and zoot suits once had their day.

We ask for freedom;
   You hand us chains.
We want tomorrows, you offer the past.
Fathers and sons, who'll be the last?
We've got to climb over this awful wall,
Or there'll be no new generation at all . . .
At all . . . at all.

As his voice disappeared in the whispered tones of the last few words, Golding's advice was forgotten, even by Golding himself. Everyone was applauding. Birdie was on her feet. Her excitement at the triumph of voice and music, of lighting and atmosphere could not be expressed sitting down. Golding and Arlen were also on their feet; the applause seemed to last for a minute, sounding louder than the sounds made by a dozen frenzied clapping hands. It was overwhelming!

Joey looked jubilant, in the knowledge that everything seemed to be working out well.

"Okay, Joey, take ten!" Golding shouted.

The magical moment vanished as the regular lights

blinked on around the room. Joey had gone back into the dressing room.

Birdie could overhear Golding and Arlen discussing Joey's performance.

"Well, what do you think, Lonny?"

"You sure know how to pick 'em, Hal. The kid's going to be a knockout. Are any of the papers coming?"

"I told *Show Business* and *Backstage* to catch the act early next week. Maybe *Variety*'ll send down their New Acts reporter."

Birdie excused herself and rushed backstage to be with Joey.

It was nine o'clock. Joey stood behind the screen, listening to the uncontrolled laughter of the audience reacting to Arlen's routine. Birdie had kept everyone from visiting him until after his first performance. Now, she was sitting out there with Papa and Lily. Many of the other tables were filled with their friends and neighbors from Gowanus who had heard about Joey and had come to lend support. Many of the ironworkers were sitting stiffly in their seats, looking uncomfortably formal in their shirts and ties, hair combed back and shiny looking. This was their own Joey, Big Joe's boy, and they were here to give him a big hand.

Joey was standing near the stove, the center of all eyes —then he sat through two numbers, as he sang. He moved naturally and gracefully, the songs pouring out without a trace of nervousness that usually comes with a first professional performance. Through the smoky haze and dim light, he could see his family, the Le Bruns, and the Marshalls, and he sang as if they were the only audience. At one point, he caught Birdie's face, aglow with pride and excitement, and he winked slightly, making her grin from ear to ear.

Back in Golding's office, after the first performance, Joey sat on the couch, feeling both tired and triumphant. He had been applauded and cheered, and whistled at, and at the end, had been given a standing ovation. But those were people he knew, people who had watched him grow up, people woven into his life like the sacred shells in a wampum belt. What did Golding think?

"How about a Coke, kid?"

"I'd rather not, Mr. Golding. I'm overheated. Better wait a bit."

"Good idea, Joey. Can't have you catching cold."

Silence.

Golding paced back and forth, came out from behind his desk.

"You've got something, Joey. I knew it when we first met. Now, I'm going to level with you. If I praise you to the skies, I'd be phony. If I tell you that you can be much better, that's closer to the truth, but it sounds depressing as hell. So I'm going to give it you Golding's way . . . straight from the shoulder. Right now, you're like a hundred other kids I've seen the past year. Green, eager to please, with talent in every finger. When I signed you, I signed you not for what you are now but for what I know you can be, in a few years. Sometimes, we patrons of the arts work on potential, you know. Like that Pope signing up Michelangelo to do the Sistine. Neither of them knew how it would turn out, and do you know, Joey, it took old Mike about eleven years, working on his back much of the time to finish that job? Well, what's that got to do with you, huh? It means this. If you work at what you've got—and I mean really work hard—I think it'll happen. You were okay tonight . . . fresh, somebody new, and they were rooting for you, even those strangers out there who never saw you before. You'll get better as the nights pass. And then the two weeks are up. You're going to need to study, Joey. To train, to vocalize, to build your voice.

"Your music is something else. Keep it going. Your ideas are good and your lyrics know where they're going, right along with your music.

"Just one more thing. If you have no plans for your summer, I'd like to get you to try summer stock, doing chorus work, or even some juvenile parts. It's a different kind of exposure, and it will do you good. And then, think about school, like the Berghof outfit, right here in the Village, or the American Academy uptown. If you're serious about a show biz career, you're not too young to get started."

It came at Joey like a barrage—words, ideas, the honesty, the sincerity, the whole final judgment of Hal Golding.

"Wow," he sighed.

"Wow, is right. I like you, Joey, and I'd like to get my kicks watching you come along, like I've watched a few others. Their names aren't important . . . and I don't want to scare you, or impress you. It's all a matter of luck . . . and persistence. I better let you go. You ought to rest before the eleven o'clock show. There's a comfortable sofa in your dressing room. Try it out for size. And I want you to know that I listened very carefully to you tonight, kid. Every single note and chord. I hope you've listened to me."

"I have, Mr. Golding."

"By the way, Joey. I almost puked when I saw that

poster outside. It's not there any more. My secretary got frantic, and I've been so busy running around about the Astronauts, I didn't get a chance to talk to Tony Parrilla, who handles my publicity. She told him you were young, good looking, and an Indian. So the jerk goes ahead and stupidly does what you saw out there. I apologize—for Tony, for my secretary, and for The Living End. We'll do you justice tomorrow. A photographer will be here at about seven. We'll get something up there . . . something good."

Joey was relieved to hear the explanation.

"Thanks, Mr. Golding. Thanks very much."

"Well now, scoot. Vamoose. Beat it."

Joey walked back to the dressing room to face the people who were eager to share his first hours as a professional performer.

Each night, during Joey's engagement, Birdie showed up at The Living End about half an hour before he was through with his performance. She would wait in the dressing-room corridor until the applause rose, signaling his closing number.

Every night it was the same. She would enter the small dressing room, they would embrace and kiss. Both found it hard to say anything those first few moments. It was still new and exciting and they hoped the happiness could last a while longer.

"How'd it go tonight?" she would ask.

"Birdie, it's been so great! Everybody's so friendly and warm. If these audiences are honest, then I can't hesitate to say that they just *like* what I'm doing—they're enjoying it!"

"I'm sure they have been."

"It's hard to put into words, Birdie, the kind of magic you feel. You hear your name announced. The noise dies down and the next minute you're out there in front of a roomful of strangers. At first, you can hear yourself. Your voice is traveling to the far ends of the room. Then slowly, it comes back, only this time it's bringing them back with it—the people out there listening. You feel it in your bones —they're with you—and when it's serious, they seem to be holding their breath. It's weird, but that audience becomes part of you and what you're doing. And it changes every night."

"Are you tired?"

"No, not the least bit. In fact, I've been reading in bed every night when I get home. It's the only way I can fall asleep, I'm so wound-up! I'm sure I've upset the family routine. You know that Mom gets up early every day to fix breakfast but she's been waiting up for me just to hear how it went. Lights at our house have been going out at about two every morning. It's awful—but they won't stop waiting up."

"They? You mean Mike, too?"

"No, not Mike. Mom and Papa."

"I shouldn't have asked, Joey. That was stupid."

"No. It's not stupid, Birdie. Mike is Mike. What else can I say?"

"He sure liked your performance on opening night."

"How do you know? Has he talked with you about it? He hasn't said a thing to me. Now there I go sounding stupid. Why should he say anything?"

"No, Joey. He hasn't spoken to me about it. But I could

tell. Even though he seemed to be sitting on his hands. He had a strange look on his face. He almost looked as though he had been defeated by something stronger than he'd ever encountered before."

"Mike . . . defeated? That's hard to believe. Anyway, Papa and Mom are enjoying every minute of it. And I know I am."

"Me too."

They would leave The Living End, making their way through the streets to the subway. The Village was always lively, especially late at night. They couldn't resist stopping here and there to window shop. Jewelry shops, displaying unique rings and bracelets; clothing shops with the latest mod fashions from London strewn casually over racks and counters; antique stores hoarding strange combinations of junk and fine, attractive Victorian pieces. Sometimes they would stop for a hamburger and coke, and then remind themselves that both families were still up, waiting for them to return.

School was another matter. Joey was tired. He knew he needed more sleep, but it was a strange, almost good sense of fatigue. His teachers seemed to conspire to make no demands on him, as though they knew that perhaps his future lay elsewhere, far away from textbooks and assignments. He was sure to make up any of the work he would postpone for two weeks. And in his classes, and in the cafeteria and the halls, there was back-slapping, hand-shaking, fingers pointing. The school had a new celebrity.

One night, after taking Birdie home, Joey found Lily waiting for him, flushed and excited.

"Joey, this letter came today. It's addressed to you.

When I saw it was from the Union, I knew it must be about the scholarship. I couldn't help myself. I hope you don't mind that I opened it. I was worried."

"Of course not, Mom. Let's see if I can guess what it says. No, don't come closer—I want to read it in your face."

Lily was smiling as she ran to her son and embraced him.

"Joey, I'm so proud of you. I—" she began to cry.

"Don't Mom . . . don't—" He found his own words blocked in his throat.

"If only your Dad could have been here to share it with us."

"Yes, I wish he were, Mom. Does Mike know about it?"

"I told him, Joey. I wondered if I ought to wait until you came home, but Papa told me not to wait. It seemed to mean something special to him, to tell Mike right away."

"What did he say?" Joey asked.

"I'm not sure. He mumbled something—sounded like 'Well, if that's what he wants.' I told him it *was* what you wanted. And then I broke down and told him it was what I wanted, too. All these years he's been hoping to have you up there with him as part of his crew. But I knew I couldn't go through that whole thing all over again. Me, waiting at home for you to come down each day, wondering if it'll happen again—to you—like it happened to Big Joe. Go, Joey. Mike's inside watching the Late Show. Speak with him. Please."

"In a minute, Mom."

Joey opened the envelope and slowly drew out the letter.

Dear Joey:

It is with great pride and pleasure that I am privileged to announce the Board's choice of Joseph Montagne, Jr., as winner of this year's John Harper Scholarship Award.

As you know, the prize pays $4,000 toward tuition for a four-year period of higher education at an institution of the winner's choice.

A committee of eminent educators chose you from a field of eleven applicants. Your outstanding scholastic record and your leadership in community youth activities have won for you the unanimous decision of the judges.

We are proud of you as a young man with a fine potential, and doubly proud that you are the son of one of our most revered friends and workers, the late Joseph Montagne.

Good luck, Joey, and the best from all of us here at the Ironworkers' Local.

Affectionately,

Sam Simpson

14

JOEY FOLDED the letter neatly and placed it back in the envelope.

"Well, I guess there's no use putting it off any longer. If Mike and I have to lock horns, I'd better get it over with."

"Don't say anything you'd be sorry for, Joey. He still is your uncle."

"I can't promise you that, Mom. He's got to be willing to take it, as well as give it."

Lily knew her son was right, and that nothing more she could say would make a difference. She smiled at Joey, a full, warm smile that made him think of some medieval noblewoman sending a loved one off to battle or to the Crusades.

The parlor doors drew slowly open. Mike turned to see who it was, then rose from his seat, and switched the television set off. Betty Grable in "Coney Island." He had seen it at least a half-dozen times. Nothing else seemed to be able to hold his attention. It was one of those barren nights in television land.

He looked at Joey. "I guess I should be congratulatin' ya." He walked from the TV toward where Joey was standing, and offered his hand. They shook hands. The physical contact was a rare event, and Mike's hand seemed to envelop Joey's. The handshake came out clumsily.

"Thanks, Mike."

Silence.

"I never told you anything the night we went to hear you sing. You were all right." Mike seemed pained; each word seemed to pause in his mouth before he released it.

"Thanks, again," Joey said. He was looking straight at Mike, challenging him to keep talking, to say things he needed to say and had kept locked up, deep inside himself.

Silence.

"Mike, do you like me?"

"What?"

"I said, do you like me?" Joey repeated.

"Now what the hell kind of question is that? You're my family, ain't ya? You're my brother's son."

"That doesn't answer my question. Do you like me? Me!"

"I don't get ya. You tryin' to tell me something?" Mike suddenly looked weak and tired, as though Joey's question had knocked a mask off his face and revealed a countenance Joey had never seen before.

"Maybe I am. Can we sit down?" Joey said.

"Sit down. It's your house too, ain't it? You sure are actin' funny."

"Ever since I can remember, I've been told I had to love you . . . you were my uncle. No one ever told me I had to love Papa . . . that he was my grandfather. I just did love him . . . naturally. And then as I grew older, I realized that nobody can make another person love somebody . . . just because they feel you're obligated to."

Mike was silent, looking down at the floor, embarrassed, as though the words Joey spoke were in a foreign tongue.

Joey continued. "I tried to do what I was told—to love you—but I guess you know and I do, too, that it wasn't easy. And then, I learned that you had to like the people you gave your love to. That was something different from loving them automatically because they were your mother, or your grandfather, or your uncle. And I found that even harder to do. To like you. And I wasn't sure it was only my fault.

"You've built some crazy steel wall around yourself, and I'm too confused and tired to even understand why. Maybe it started when my father died. I know you loved him. Maybe you couldn't cope with your feeling of loss. I don't know.

"Or maybe it started when you began to take his place around here. I never figured that one out, either. Whether you wanted to take his place, or needed to take his place. Or whether Papa and Lily gave you a role to play—a role you weren't ready for. Anyway, I want to tell you that I don't hate you, and that I just feel sorry that we couldn't have gotten to know each other better . . . and understand each other more. I guess that's all I have to say . . . except that I want to hear you respond. Now. Don't dismiss me by going for a beer, or walking out. Please."

Mike walked to the fireplace, stood staring into it, as though the charred opening held the ashes of some dark secret.

"Maybe you're right, kid. I guess nobody oughta try to

do something they can't. Like you bein' an ironworker. Like me trying to take your father's place." He was trying to make his thoughts clear. He spoke slowly. "I was sure you'd be as good as your father some day. Now that I think about it, I don't know how the hell I ever got that idea. You just don't have the same stuff in you that Big Joe had. You never will."

Joey had to interrupt. "But that was wrong. Can't you see that? He was what he was. And I'm me. We're different. You make it sound like a sin. You had no right to expect that I'd be another Big Joe."

"I dunno, Joey. I think he mighta been ashamed . . . like I am. One thing we Montagnes never counted on was havin' a streak of yellow runnin' across our name. Ya understand?"

"Yellow? That's a laugh. What makes you think standing in front of a room filled with strangers, singing your heart out, is any easier than what you guys do up on the beams? Sure, what you do is more dangerous, and maybe a million times harder . . . but there are many kinds of bravery, Mike."

"What did you think I was trying to do to you, Joey . . . by makin' ya an ironworker—like your father, like Papa? Did you think I was tryin' to kill ya?"

Joey hesitated. "The ways in which people kill each other, Mike, don't have to be dramatic. They can be slow and quiet. They can murder with indifference, or with stupidity. You've been doing it to me ever since my father died. You shut me out of your life . . . only wanting to accept me on your own terms. Treating me as though I wasn't worth anything because I didn't see the world your way."

The words pounded away at Mike, like a dozen rivet guns driving into the hidden places in his soul where nothing had ever touched before. His face showed the pain. For an instant he found himself unable to speak. He walked to a chair, dropping into it as though he might find a place to hide. His voice came out of some hollow corner of his chest as though it were not his own.

"Joey—I've never told this to your mother, or anyone else. Listen to me, please. That day, when Big Joe fell— it was a lousy day. It rained that morning, and it was windy as hell. It wasn't easy workin' up there. We all knew it, and when we got the order to come down, we were all glad. That's when the stupid betting begins—to see which crew would be the last to come down. We'd done it dozens of times before. Your father knew it was dangerous, but he had to play the game, like everybody. Our crew *had* to be the last one down. It was crazy, kid stuff, but it was always like that. The Montagnes had to be the best."

Joey realized he was hearing some sort of confession that only Mike and himself were fated to share.

"There was somethin' inside your father—like a devil drivin' him to show the others that us Caughnawagas were the best. Stayin' up there, walkin' in the sky, fightin' the world was another way to show 'em. Well, it was slippery that day and I shoulda stayed up there with Big Joe—or I shoulda made him come down with me. I told him we'd win the bet, to stay up just a little longer. When he fell, I couldn't believe it. The wind picked him off the beam like he was made of straw. I've never stopped hearin' that scream as he fell—it wasn't Big Joe's voice. It was a strange sound, like a kid, a baby wailin' at night a block away. When I got to the ground, they wouldn't let me see him or touch him. It seemed like a year 'til the ambulance came. But I knew he was dead. They all knew—and I cursed them all. And I cursed Big Joe for dying. I cursed him and his game . . . and I wished it was me smashed up instead of him. I still wish it had been me."

Joey knew how hard it must have been for Mike to say the words he'd just heard. He also knew he couldn't say anything, at this moment, which would have meaning for Mike, or help him to dispel the weight of the guilt he'd been carrying through the years.

As they sat together in deep silence, Joey thought, "He really wanted me to be there with him, to take Big Joe's place—to make him feel that the accident had never happened, and that Big Joe was still there."

Joey wanted to run out of the room, away from Mike, away from the house—to be alone where he could think . . . and cry.

Walking in the sky.

That's what Mike had said . . . walkin' in the sky, fightin' the world. What right had any man to think he was a god? Icarus beating his wings against the sun, falling to earth like Big Joe. Didn't his father's shattered remains prove that even men like Mike and Papa, and Henry Riviere and younger men like Buzz Gallagher and Billy Le Brun were not made of rivets and bolts and steel.

He felt the tears come, and he was not ashamed, in front of Mike. Poor Mike, who probably had dried the springs in his soul where tears could start. All his years of rain and wind and sun and heat.

Who was yellow now?

Joey looked at his uncle, and wordlessly rose and left the room.

15

Soon after the news of Joey's scholarship, Thora Marshall decided it would be a fine idea to celebrate it with a party. Not only the scholarship. Joey's career had been launched with his two-week engagement at The Living End. Birdie's research project would soon reach its culmination. And most satisfying of all, her meeting with the women in the neighborhood had begun to show results. Like an army of ants, with Father Bello and Jim, who had gotten permission to make temporary repairs, they had boarded up the broken windows, removed the paint stains, and cleaned up and restored the furniture. One of the husbands had painted in huge letters on the front—OUR BUSINESS IS YOUR FUTURE. And in the last few days, eighteen youngsters had shown up for tutoring.

The Marshall apartment in the Village was small, and Thora knew she would have to limit the guests to about eight couples. She talked with Birdie about whom to invite, and they narrowed their list down to people they knew Joey would enjoy spending the evening with—some from the cast of *The Fantasticks*, Billy Le Brun and his date, and Joey and herself.

"What do you kids like to eat?" Thora asked Birdie.

"That's a dangerous question, Mrs. Marshall. You know, the usual stuff. Pizza, delicatessen. Just as long as there's a lot of it. You know kids. We never stop eating."

"Well, I'm glad I asked, anyway. Since my husband is in his own way responsible for some small part of your education, I thought I'd make my own contribution. Birdie, polish off your castanets. We are going to have one of my good, old-fashioned southern Spanish dinners, from *sopa* to nuts."

"Sounds great, Mrs. Marshall. And it sure will be educational. I don't think any of us has ever eaten Spanish food."

"Well, if we're going to be authentic, it'll be served real late. I thought we might do it, as a surprise, after Joey's closing performance. We thought we'd all go down there, as guests of Jim and myself, and then come back to our apartment afterwards. It's only a short walk."

"Can I help you, Mrs. Marshall?"

"Don't be silly, Birdie. The whole dinner comes right over from a neighborhood restaurant. You don't think I'm going to stand over a hot stove all day Sunday, my day of rest. And anyway, I could never do as good a job as they do. Wait and see."

Ten o'clock, Sunday night found all the guests waiting at the Marshalls' apartment for Birdie and Joey.

Thora and Jim knew they wouldn't be serving any alcohol, so Thora settled for an imitation sangria made with grape juice, which looked and tasted like the genuine

Spanish wine punch. Since there was no space for a sit-down meal, they had decided to lay out a buffet.

A huge paella had been delivered, together with enough salad and delicious bread to serve eighteen or twenty guests. The large paella platter had to be kept warm, but it wouldn't fit in the stove, so Thora finally propped the stove door ajar in order to accommodate it. She didn't want to ruin the luscious appearance of the dish, with its saffron rice and small slices of red and green peppers giving it the look of a large, exotic flower. The odor of the cooked chicken, the pink-tinged shrimp, the sausage, and the clams and mussels spread through the apartment. Appetites were running high because of the tempting smells and the late hour.

"They should be here any minute," Thora assured everybody.

Billy Le Brun, sitting on the floor at the feet of his steady girl, Agnes Reilly, sipped the sangria and complained, "I don't know how much longer I'm gonna be able to wait. I'm starving."

"Good things come to him who waits," said Agnes. "That's what my mother always says. Or is it 'he who waits,' Mr. Marshall?"

"Uh-uh, none of that stuff tonight, Agnes. You're not going to catch me correcting grammar. I guess that's an occupational hazard. Every time someone finds out I'm an English teacher, they immediately shift gears and try to keep from making mistakes. The heck with that. Billy, I know how you feel. My stomach's been sending me messages for the past half-hour."

"You men," chided Thora, "always thinking of your

stomachs. You can't begin to eat before our guests of honor arrive."

Ben La Marca, who had been a stagehand for "The Fantasticks" but had since quit school to help his ailing father run a small grocery store in the neighborhood, walked around the living room looking at the paintings which formed a gallery wall behind the sofa and wherever wall space allowed. He pointed to a colorful abstract oil painting, all swirls and angles.

"Mrs. Marshall, where'd this one come from? What does it mean?"

"I don't know that it means anything, Ben. It's just an abstract impression of the island of Ibiza, off Spain. I liked the colors and the texture, and I bought it—or rather Jim bought it for me for our anniversary two years ago. We took one of those three-week Spanish tours, and I guess we got hooked on almost anything Spanish. Do you like it?"

"I dunno," Ben said. "I guess I like pictures I understand, better. It doesn't look like an island to me, just a bunch of triangles on top of one another."

Billy spoke up from his place on the floor. "You oughta see Manhattan from the top of one of the Verrazano towers! It looks just like that. A bunch of angles, and stuff like we used to study in geometry."

Ben wandered past the wall of books from floor to ceiling. "You sure have got a lotta books," he said, examining the bookshelves.

"Both of us read a lot, Ben, but we've got to be careful. We've stopped buying fiction. There's just not that much room anymore on the shelves."

Ben looked serious. "It sure is a nice apartment. I've

never been to a Negro's home before." It had slipped out.

"Oh?" Thora asked. "And what did you expect?"

"Excuse me, Mrs. Marshall, I didn't mean nothin' bad," he said, blushing. "It's just the fact that this is the first time I've ever been a guest of a colored person." Innocently, Ben was still unaware that his remarks had shot through the group like a small thunderbolt.

Thora smiled. "I accept that fact, Ben, and all the honesty that goes with it, but it's a little hard to go along with the buried prejudice. I suppose many people would expect to see African masks hanging on our walls, and they'd also expect us to serve chitlins' and black-eyed peas on a large chunk of watermelon. But it really doesn't work that way, Ben. You see, although Jim and I aren't willing to forget we're black, there are lots of people who make sure we don't forget—every chance they get. If you like this apartment then, in a way, you're saying you like us, and that's all that counts. I wish there were more people who are willing to take human beings as they are—just as humans, rather than *this* color human, or *that*." Thora's passion made her eyes flash with indignation.

The sudden sound of the door buzzer reduced the tension like the gong between rounds at a prize fight. Jim was relieved, as he rushed to open the door for the late arrivals.

Birdie and Joey were surrounded at the door and drowned in the noise of the warm greetings thrown at them from every side.

"Birdie, did you know this was going to happen?" Joey asked.

"Can't say I didn't."

"Fink." He turned to the Marshalls. "How wonderful you both are, for thinking of me this way!"

Jim Marshall responded with, "The older you get, the more you'll realize that some of the best hours of your life are spent with people you really want to be with. Can I lead you two to the punch bowl? This way!"

Birdie and Joey were finally settled on the sofa. Billy asked Joey how he felt on his closing night.

"I really don't know yet, Billy. I haven't even had time to think about it. I know it's been the greatest experience of my life, and I'm sorry to see it end."

The room was quiet with a momentary depression.

"If you'll permit me to be the wise old man I am," Marshall smiled, "I'd like to pass this on to you, Joey. My father used to tell it to me, especially around Christmas time, when we were putting the tinsel and stuff away for the following year. He told us that the end of one thing really meant the beginning of something else, that there would be lots of other Christmases to come. I couldn't understand what he meant too well, then. But never let the ending of something good in your life sadden you. It's really the beginning of another chance to let some other good things come along."

"Listen to him, will you?" Thora kidded. "A philosopher on an empty stomach."

"Speaking of empty stomachs . . ." Billy repeated.

"Young man, I hear you loud and clear," Thora told him.

"How can you keep these red-blooded American youngsters from their rightful heritage—good old Spanish food?" Jim chuckled.

"Red-blooded?" quipped Thora. "Are you sure? That's a bad joke, kids, in case you've never heard one."

While Jim put a Rodrigo guitar concerto into the record player, Thora served the paella and salad, with heaps of the crisp bread. The room was filled with the sounds of dishes being passed, platters, and silverware and the tinkling of ice cubes in glasses. Then, slowly, the sounds subsided as everybody settled back in hushed contentment. When it was time for dessert, Thora announced, "Now listen, all of you. I've got the simplest dessert I could think of, a chilled fresh mango for each of us. It gives me a chance to show off the special mango forks we picked up in Mexico a few years ago. Down there, we had to be shown how to use them, but if you'll all watch Jim, he'll give you a lesson in how to devour these divine and, incidentally, expensive mangoes."

As they gathered to watch Jim, prepared to imitate him, Joey realized that this was his very first Spanish dinner, his first taste of a mango. Marshall was right. Life was filled with beginnings, new experiences that followed so quickly after one another, you could not waste time thinking about or brooding about the past. He thought about Lily and what she would do with her life, and about Papa, who seemed so genuinely glad to be alive each day. He thought about Birdie and himself and the mysterious directions in which their lives might be headed. And he wondered about Mike, and if it might be the beginning of a new understanding between them.

In the glow of the candlelight from the table, he looked around at the room filled with people who had given him friendship and loyalty. The soft guitar concerto seemed a fitting background for the way in which his heart seemed to be singing. He reached for Birdie's hand and let it rest gently in his own.

Epilogue

T<small>HE</small> <small>AISLES OF</small> St. Paul's were crowded with ironworkers and their families, but what impressed Joey even more than the large turnout was the awesome silence of these men whose usual attitude was noisy, boisterous, and good-natured.

Lily, Mike, and Papa sat near the front of the church. The sun filtering through the stained glass tossed crystal reflections across the altar and the vases of huge, white chrysanthemums standing on either side.

The choir began its solemn chant. Lily's eyes filled with tears as she remembered the service for Big Joe at the reservation, and she shared, once more, the deep empty feeling of loss with the families of the dead men—families sitting all around the church and remembering with her, as they listened to the comforting music.

After the Mass, Father Bello stepped forward and spoke in a clear, resonant voice.

"Dear friends, there is really so little I can say in the way of paying tribute to the men we have come here to honor today. I would rather share my thought that their strength, their noble skill, stand out there in the harbor; that their blood and muscle have mingled with the steel—to defy the elements for as long as the bridge shall stand. In an age when man is so lost in a technological maze, that bridge is a miracle—a miracle of pride and love, shared by all the men who put their bodies and souls into the finishing of that task.

"There is a young man among us who, like David the minstrel, has asked to stand before you, to let his voice and heart tell you what we all must feel on this occasion."

Joey, dressed in a dark suit, rose and walked forward from the front pew where he had been sitting with Birdie. For this occasion, he had tied black ribbons which now dangled from the neck of his guitar, for the men who had been killed during the building of the bridge. Standing near one of the white bouquets, he looked out over the faces of the men and the families he knew so well.

Like a madrigal, his new song floated toward the rear of the building, hitting the gothic arches, reverberating to the altar. The words he sang told of the challenge these men had accepted—to go where man had not gone, to fight the wind, the cold, and the height, to create something where nothing before had existed, to fill a natural void with a monument to the genius of man. The words, the music, the title told it all—"Walk in the Sky."

Birdie watched and listened and was proud of him. The rays of light pouring through the stained glass windows of the church, the flowers and the flickering candles seemed to melt into one glowing pattern. It reminded her of an old Indian blanket her grandmother had once shown her, which had been passed on to the women in her family for many generations. Its colors were soft and muted, like the interior of the old church.

When his song was finished, Joey walked slowly back to the pew where Birdie sat.

It was one of those rare moments when everyone seemed to sense that nothing more could be added to make the occasion more beautiful or complete. Slowly, the worshippers rose and strode toward the exit.

Mike had offered Lily his arm, and they walked up the aisle together. Papa walked behind them.

Already, the men had begun to talk in excited whispers about the rumor of a new skyscraper, a World Trade Center—alleged to be even higher than the Empire State Building.

Joey and Birdie made their way up to the roof of the Montagne house. Although they couldn't see it, they knew that the Verrazano-Narrows Bridge was out there and, like the other buildings and bridges in the city, in a way, it was all their very own.

ABOUT THE AUTHOR

JACK ISHMOLE, a native New Yorker, teaches English, radio broadcasting and film production to young people at a junior high school on Long Island.

Directing community theatre productions, collecting art, and visiting the sites of ancient civilizations often give him the chance to experience interesting people and places.

His interest in the Mohawks led him to research the exploits of the "building and bridge warriors" and the idea for WALK IN THE SKY. Previously he edited an anthology for young people, NEW YORK PORTRAIT: A Literary Look at the Empire State.

He lives in the shadow of the new World Trade Center with two dogs and a fascinating collection of neighbors.